The Chalk Canoe

A Cat McCloud Book

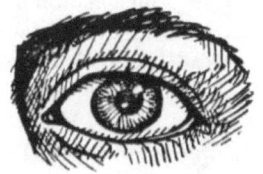

Heidi Arneson

ISBN-13: 978-0997477818
ISBN-10: 0997477814

Published in 2019 by Stick Pony Press,
an imprint of Invisible Ink, Minneapolis, Minnesota.
Inquiries may be directed to rachel@rmapublicity.com

For Miriam Arneson (1922-2017)
and Alberta Mirais

Part One

The Dream of a Happy Childhood

ONE

I'd laugh, if laughing didn't quicken my death.

I'm belly-deep in muck under all the waters of Little Rose Lake with a thousand crayfish nibbling at my buried parts and a jumbo snapping turtle about to bite off my face. The snapper's sharp jaws are open, his angry eyes are closed, and even if they could find me in these murky depths, none of the neighbor kids could pull me from this muck-hole.

You know that feeling like you're dying when you're really only just waking up? That pain in your pumper like your insides are about to turn inside out and the dams of your arteries are about to give way, and all that you've been holding in is about to explode into the unknown? Death has a taste. It bubbles up from the inside, black and green, thick and sour, a grainy mush. I almost drowned once before, when the bratty twins who couldn't swim used me as a ladder, so I know how death-by-drowning feels. The white circle of water closing over, your last look at sky, that delicious fishy smell and the silent scream that brings in more water. And I've tasted death in my dreams, in the back of my throat while cleaning out the endlessly overflowing public toilets of Sleepland. But this is real life I'm talking about. In real life when death spills out of you in a pudding mush, then you know you were carrying death around inside you all that time. You were letting death walk upright inside you.

I used to think death was on the outside waiting for me. I used to think death was waiting around the corner as I toddled from our bedroom and my sister Holly jumped out and yelled BOO! I'd jump as high as a toddler could then Holly ran to the next corner and BOO and to the next and BOO! At every corner Holly waited like death trying to scare me out of my rubber pants. And death was in our copper oven with the clock behind the clouded glass stopped forever from a summer thunderstorm. Holly and Tammy would preheat that oven, set me on a cookie sheet, salt and pepper me and carry me to the open oven door— and though they never put me in, I always knew the last thing I would see in my short life was that oven light. And death was in the grocery bag full of kittens my big brothers held tight to the station wagon exhaust before I was born because Mom was pregnant with me and cats made pregnant women sick. And death was in the pillow Tammy held over my face after I was born because I was why those kittens died.

One, two, three, four, five dead kittens. Six, seven, eight, nine, ten living kids. When you're the baby of ten in a house full of life you better learn fast how to disappear because death is waiting around every corner. Death in the pinchers of the spiders in our step crack silently weaving their eggs sacs, death behind the basement bathroom tiles, atop my big sisters' dresser, and in the stillness of the milk glasses on the supper table before Dad's explosion turned our stomachs upside-down.

To get away from all that death I'd sit down by the lake and make wishes. *Let me fly like in my dreams. Let me turn into a real-live mermaid. Let the cute boy love me. Let the bratty twins dry up and die if they sass me one more time! And let the waters of Little Rose Lake be sucked up in a giant whirlwind so the bottom is laid bare.* LET THE BOTTOM BE LAID BARE! I imagined all the waters drawn up in a maelstrom. Stringbean Tomboy shared my wish. We ached to wade through the newly-exposed muck and explore the lake's history. The lake was clean, because it was spring-fed, but greenish-black muck clouded everything. When we bellied down on Andersons' dock and peered in, or dove off our raft and looked up, all we saw was sunlight shooting through yellow-green. What else, we wondered, besides my big sisters' wedding rings, Stringbean's lost hockey pucks, and the Blakes' sunken Evinrude lay hidden in the muck? Were there peat-blackened pig bones from the old stockyards and rocks round as skulls from the crumbling ice house? Were there rusted trucks like the old Ford haunting Highlook Meadow? Or were there deeper relics hidden in that muck? Were there dinosaur bones big as the bulldozers digging up our vacant lots? Or curled bodies of ancient people? Or dangers from another time waiting to unfurl evil curses? I imagined myself in Mr. Anderson's waders, slogging through the empty lake-bed, pulling up grotesque treasures, a baby-doll, a rusty stroller, a screaming skull—

This summer my wish came true and it's about to kill me, with a huge snapping turtle inches from my face.

TWO

It started with the crack at the bottom of our front steps. A ragged gap in the cement ran across the bottom like a mouth filled with dead leaves and who-knows-what. That crack was one of the dangerous places where you were never supposed to reach. *Don't peek under the bed, don't look atop that dresser, and never put your fingers in the crack at the bottom of our front steps.* In there were sticky cobwebs and biting spiders, and in there the undead lay waiting to suck your soul out your fingertips.

That crack got wider every year, separating our house from the yard. I imagined one day our house would go sliding down into the lake. When that happened we'd go on as before. We'd pretend our house wasn't sliding in. We'd get so good at pretending we'd be blind to the slow-moving evidence, like the tiny scars on Mom's hands—always there, never talked about.

When the crack reached the tulip bed, something else would take our attention, a task in the garage, someone calling our name, or the supper dishes, and we'd forget all about that expanding crack. It would be just a bad feeling. We'd get the bad feeling, but we wouldn't know from what. Impending doom, yes, but from where? When that crack gaped into the basement and critters scampered in, ants, mice, and snakes, we'd keep making supper, keep watching TV, keep drying the dishes. Because what do you do when your whole life is sliding toward doom?

Nothing. You do nothing. You walk around with that bad feeling and carry on. There was no sticking your fingers in that crack, no getting down on your hands and knees and peering in. Every time we McClouds stepped down our front steps we stepped right over.

Not till my thirteenth year, in the coldest spring in White Rock, on my last day of sixth grade, did I see anyone stick their fingers in that crack. Maybe that person didn't know any better. Maybe she was oblivious. Maybe she was too new for the unspoken rules. Or maybe she knew she was breaking a rule, and that was why she did it.

Dee-dee Morton was the cool new older girl. She was two whole years older. She moved from the city with her mom, dad, and little brother Robbie. Dee-dee had long golden locks that hid her face. Her woman-sized breasts moved freely inside her olive green sweater. Her bare feet wore her bellbottoms to shreds as she scuffed our neighborhood looking for mystery, and two dabs of saliva gathered at the corners of her mouth as she talked to me in her throaty whisper, as if she and I were alone together in three hundred sixty degrees of ancient mystery.

Why had Dee-dee befriended me? I wasn't cool, rich, or dangerous. Perhaps it was our driftwood. Every other house on Little Rose Lake Road had a store-bought lawn ornament, reflective blue sphere, landscape boulder, ceramic figurine. But my uncle's abandoned Chevy Blazer rusted by our driveway, our backyard had a handmade birdhouse towering thirty feet up on a slender wooden post, and our front yard had weathered twists of driftwood Mom had gathered on the Mississippi. Small twists, medium twists, and large twists leaned against our house and writhed in our garden like trapped spirits. One tree root embracing our mailbox stood taller than Dad, its many arms going every which way.

On the day Dee-dee Morton walked down our street looking for mystery, that driftwood opened its silvery mouth and called out, Dee-dee Morton! Dee-dee Morton! Cool New Older Girl! Walk across this lawn! Step over this crack! Ring this bell! For here resides mystery! Dee-dee crossed our lawn, stepped over the crack, and rang our bell. No one else was home, so I sucked the blood from my freshly-cut finger, brushed myself off, and opened the door to a head of gold hair with no face.

Pale fingers parted the hair, revealing whirlpool-blue eyes and rosebud lips. From the lips came a throaty whisper.

"What's that driftwood for?"

"It's my mom's," I said. "She's not home."

I tried to shut the door but too late. Dee-dee had spied my sister's sparkly dioramas, Mom's abstract quilts of nature entangled in silent ecstasy, and my bloody hand, so she pawed her way in asking, "What is this? Who made that? What is that?"

I just shrugged.

Then she cast her blue whirlpools on me, "Who are you?"

She wasn't asking *who are you* as in name, age, and grade. She was asking a deeper *who are you*. She was asking the *who are you* Dad was asked at his Briefcase Carrier's Conference for Deeper Self Awareness. Dad brought those questions home, and after three martinis he shared them with me at the dining room table with his smoke rising and his ice clinking, as a gentle reminder for me to have a deeper self-awareness of myself:

WHO ARE YOU?
WHAT ARE YOU DOING?
WHAT DO YOU WANT TO BE DOING?

I went right to my room and answered in my Peter Max spiral notebook with a purple Flair felt-tip.

> *I'm a body composed of billions of cells. Each cell is an independent being. You can isolate one in a petri dish and it will fight to live all by itself, but each cell serves the whole, and all together they make up the universe of seeing, feeling, thinking ME. I see with my eyes, I feel with my nerves, I hear with my ears. Light hits the rods and cones of my retina and an image is projected upside-down, then my brain turns it right-side up and puts it into words that chop the universe into tiny chewable bits: Mom, Dad, house, lake, tree, etc.*

I couldn't write the entire WHO ARE YOU in that moment, for how can you write the complexity of your infinite insides without getting a hand cramp? You can't. So when Dee-dee Morton asked, "who are you?" I just shrugged. That's how our friendship began. No phone calls, no plans. Dee-dee would just show up after school, step out from behind my uncle's old Chevy Blazer, and say in her throaty whisper, "Hi Cat, how are you doing?"

THREE

On my last day of sixth grade I fought the wind all the way home, past the bratty twins playing catch in the street, Mrs. Zupinski biking by with her flyers, and Mr. and Mrs. Anderson out digging in their garden. They were all doing springtime things but spring hadn't come to White Rock yet.

It was the record-breaking endless winter of 1973. The ice was still on the lake, the green beaks of our tulips still waited underground, and the wind cut right through my Superman shirt as I dropped my school stuff in our front hall and went back out for the mail—Red Owl flyer, Minnegasco bill, and a letter for Tammy with no return address or stamp.

Tammy doesn't live here anymore, I thought.

Just then Dee-dee Morton stepped out from behind the Chevy Blazer and spoke in her throaty whisper.

"Hi Cat, how are you doing?"

I shrugged. She had on that green sweater again. Her breasts were moving around inside and her blond locks obscured her face as she bent to the crack at the bottom of our front steps.

"There is something in there, Cat."

Before I could scream *don't put your hand in there*, Dee-dee put her hand in nonchalantly as if reaching into a school desk.

I expected her to jerk her fingers out throbbing with a spider bite or dripping with blood.

Instead she calmly fished around in that unknown darkness and drew out a folded piece of paper.

Her hands shook as she slowly unfolded the paper, brought it to her nose, and sniffed.

"It is perfumed, Cat. There is writing. I cannot make it out."

She thrust the note at me.

I dared take it.

The yellowed paper was soft as skin, crumpled and smoothed, and scented with some grandma's old perfume. Mercurochrome-colored words lurched across the page in sickly fountain-pen peaks and panicked curlicues.

"I can't read it either."

"Try your best," Dee-dee whispered. "Try your very best."

Try my best?

I was always trying my best! Best at math, best at attracting boys, best at acting normal, and best at carving chalk canoes. Where did it get me? Eraser holes torn in my homework, boys barking at me, and a bloody pile of broken chalk canoes. Whatever I touched I ruined.

But Dee-dee implored me with her blue whirlpools.

"Go on, Cat. I know you can do it."

I moved to the side of our house for privacy, squinted and read. "Deare Yee Who finde Thiss."

Water-splats had smeared some of the words. Someone cried over this, I thought, someone wept, some long-ago woman in a low-cut velvet dress rubbed it over her heaving chest as her tears fell, splat, to the page.

And the words were spelled dear, *deare,* and find, *finde.*

"Whoever wrote this couldn't spell."

"That is Olde English, Cat. Back then you could spell however you wanted. And spell differently every time. Read on."

A gust of wind shivered the page as I read on.

"Heed Mee with all Your Heart, I sorely hope & pray."

That's all the further I got. *I sorely hope & pray.*

Just then my high school sister Holly appeared in her hot pink mini dress, suntan pantyhose, and clunky buckle shoes.

Holly was the last sister left at home and she considered it her duty to boss me.

Before Holly could put her hands on her hips and shout her endless to-do list, SCRUB the FLOOR, WASH the DISHES, CLEAN the GARAGE, I hissed, "Dee-dee, run!"

With the yellowed note pinched between my fingers we dashed through Andersons' backyard, climbed the next neighbor's chain-link fence and cut across Little Rose Lake Road headed for Dee-dee's house, where Holly would not follow us, *we sorely hoped and prayed...*

As Dee-dee put her hand on the doorknob of her olive green split-level I swallowed. I'd never been inside Dee-dee's house before. It was the same style as Laura, Laurel, and Lori's houses, same windows, same door, same sparkly rocks in the façade, but Dee-dee's house had stood empty for years. No one lived in it till Dee-Dee moved in. For years the windows were blank, every hopeful buyer hurried away with a scared face, and the neighbors asked, what was wrong with that house? Did the basement flood? Did it have poor drainage? Were there cracks in the foundation?

No, the basement didn't flood, it didn't have poor drainage, and there were no cracks in the foundation. Dee-dee's house was the same as all the other split-levels on our street.

So why had it stood empty?

Only I knew.

Seven years before, bulldozers tore up all the vacant lots on our end of Little Rose Lake Road. All but one. At six years old I claimed the last vacant lot as my own. I ruled that lot. It was MINE. I knew every mound and gully, every stone, flowering weed, yellow buttercup, and foamy spitball hiding every green worm. In that vacant lot I gathered the little neighbor girls, fed them graham crackers, and sheltered them in dugouts roofed with discarded plywood. In my vacant lot. Of which I was Queen. The only place I was Queen. At home my family turned into monsters, but in my vacant lot I happily reigned, surrounded by my friends, the weeds, rivulets, and stones. Then one windy day in the early spring I wandered alone in my queendom and found a wooden stake stuck in the ground. One stake. Then another. I pulled up the stake, then the other, then found another. I pulled up all the stakes and took them home to Mother. What does this mean, I asked by holding out the muddy stakes. That means, Mom said, that a nice family is going to move into that vacant lot. My body formed one giant question mark. That means, Mom elaborated, a bulldozer will flatten the land, tear up the trees, and build a nice house with perhaps a playmate for you. RUINED! I was RUINED! My kingdom was to be flattened! Every beloved weed, gully, and sapling! This was worse than the loss of my toddler bed! This was my land! I went back to that lot, formed those stakes into a circle, stood in the middle, and with the wind in my hair and my hand-me-down jacket flapping, I stomped my feet, raised my arms, and called down all the powers of the Sky, called up all the powers of the Earth, Stones, Trees, Wind, Lightning, Rain, RAGE! My six year old throat, six year old heart, and the ancient powers in my six year old fists cursed the bulldozers, cement pourers, block-layers, nail-pounders ALL! I cursed them and cursed the family who would move in to an INFINITY of UNHAPPINESS.

Little did I know that would be Dee-dee's house.

Dee-dee opened the door.

I followed her in.

Six steps led up to the living room, dining room, and kitchen, then the stairs turned right, and six more steps led up to the bedrooms and bathroom. It was a normal house, newly moved in. Down in the entry, a door at the far end led to the basement, where three months later, I would find the body.

Dee-dee's little brother Robbie sat in the living room watching Star Trek on TV.

Robbie had been in Mr. Swanson's sixth grade with me. Robbie had the same sweetheart face, rosebud lips, and golden hair as Dee-dee, but Robbie was always crying. As he sat at his desk, or sat alone at lunch, or stood apart in gym, silent tears rolled down his cheeks. Robbie was cute enough to be a prince in a castle daydream, but the thought of kissing those lips below a nose ever-dripping with snot was not a good fantasy.

We turned our backs on Robbie and went up to Dee-dee's

room. On her door was a black-and-white poster of the silent film star Theda Bara hovering before an ancient Egyptian tomb. Below Theda Bara were the dripping red words, *ABANDON HOPE ALL YE WHO ENTER HERE.*

I abandoned hope and entered.

We had to duck.

From every inch of Dee-dee's ceiling something hung— fisherman's nets, psychedelically-painted Barbie-doll parts, macramé, dried wildflowers, wind chimes, glass beads, brass bells, origami birds, and tiny mammal skulls.

Above Dee-dee's bed was a dried bat tacked to the wall with its wings spread. Here and there melted candles dripped down basketed wine flasks atop stacks of books, books, and more books—*The History of Witchcraft, Common Household Spells, The Egyptian Book of the Dead.*

On the bed someone very skinny lay prone, completely covered head-to-foot in a white sheet. At their sheeted feet glared the furriest Persian gray cat I'd ever seen.

On the floor of the open closet were a pillow, a rumpled blanket, and a small lamp.

Dee-dee sat on the floor by her closet.

I sat on the floor with my back to her bed.

From the closet Dee-dee drew out a cigar box. From the cigar box she pieced together what I sorely hoped and prayed was not a marijuana cigarette. I'd never smoked the real thing before. Stringbean and I had smoked pine needles from the Andersons' fir trees, but to no effect.

Dee-dee lit, dragged deeply, and handed the smoking thing to me, "Go ahead Cat."

How could I tell her I was already high on life? And that if I took any smoke into my lungs my brain would flower with endless imaginings?

I shrugged, took the thing, and pretended to inhale.

As I coughed out smoke, Dee-dee reached into the closet for a Dixie cup and a jug of Mogen David Grape Wine. The wine she glugged into the cup, then shaved marijuana ash in, tweezed a pinch of fur from the dead bat on the wall and dropped that in, reached under the bedsheet, scraped something off the foot of whoever was under and added that to the cup, all the while chanting, "Eye of newt and toe of frog, wool of bat and tongue of dog, adder's fork and blind worm's sting!"

She thrust the cup at me.

"Drink up, Cat."

I went cross-eyed staring at the floating things in that cup, but would do whatever Dee-dee commanded. I tilted and gulped. The Mogen David, marijuana ash, bat fuzz, and whatever else flowed down my throat.

Dee-dee waved her arms, proclaiming, "NOW YOU ARE ONE OF US!"

She drew back the sheet.

The cat leapt from the bed. The dangling things above tinkled and swayed. The window blinds jerked, letting in strips of light. Upon seeing who was under that sheet, I threw the cup into the closet, where the remains hit the back wall and dripped down, leaving a purple stain.

I blinked before I screamed.

FOUR

Under that sheet was the caramelized body of a starved person, naked but for a strip of yellowed linen stuck to its thigh, with rigid limbs, brown skin shrunk tight to the bone, empty eyeholes in shriveled lids, a nose dried to a crooked peak, a mouth cringing over tiny teeth, and a bit of beef jerky between its legs.

After screaming I fainted.

I left my body, floated up through Dee-dee's dangly ceiling, over her roof, high enough to see the housetops, Highlook Meadow with the haunted Ford truck, frozen Little Rose Lake, the freeway wall, a few cars zooming, and the long, snaking body of Big Snake Lake beyond with its public beach, where come summer, pimply boys and protuberant girls would throng with their dangerous flirting.

Down in Dee-dee's room she parted her hair, bent forward, and put her lips to mine in a passionate kiss.

At the touch of Dee-dee's lips I snapped back in my body. I was kissing a halved peach, cut open and dripping. Dee-dee's hair was in my face, her breath was in my lungs, and a red-hot wire ran from her mouth to my hips.

Oh no, I thought, girls in White Rock aren't allowed to kiss other girls. Now I'm in serious trouble!

But as Dee-dee drew away I realized her kiss wasn't a kiss. She'd only been giving me mouth-to-mouth resuscitation.

She tucked her hair behind her ears.

"Cat, are you okay?"

No, I'm not okay—

You've got a real-live mummy on your bed and I'm about to faint again and this time you'll have to wake me with a real kiss.

But I just shrugged.

She grabbed my wrist and tugged me to the kitchen.

Your cat needs a comb-out, I thought as we sat in Dee-dee's kitchen eating cereal from sample boxes of Cap'n Crunch.

It was the first Cap'n Crunch anyone on our block had ever tasted. Dee-dee said that on the day the mailman delivered the free samples of Brand New Cereal, she'd been home sick, and spied through her window the mailman shoving blue and orange boxes in every mailbox, so she ran out in her nightgown with a pillowcase, and as soon as the mail truck was out of sight she stuffed her pillowcase full of Cap'n Crunch.

"Weren't you scared of getting caught?"

"Underage," Dee-dee said, "Not sixteen yet."

I put another square in my mouth. It was tasty. It was DELICIOUS. It was all the box said it would be. I let the Cap'n Crunch dissolve on my tongue as the Persian purred on my leg.

The sugar emboldened me.

"Your cat needs a comb-out," I said aloud.

"Divorce," Dee-dee said. Silent tears flowed into her cereal. "My parents are getting a divorce."

I swallowed without chewing.

Divorce?

People on our street didn't get divorced. It was unheard of. Divorce was a broken home, a dirty word, a house cracked in half, fallen on its side with darkness seeping out. Anything could happen in the horrors of a broken home. Parents, however unhappy, stayed together in White Rock. Many nights I'd woken to Dad screaming, I'M LEAVING! as he staggered to the closet and pulled out the butterscotch luggage, bellowing, no one loves me in this house! You don't love me! The kids don't love me! Everyone hates me! And Mom in her nightgown begging, no dear don't go! I love you, the kids love you, we all love you, as we kids huddled around corners sobbing, afraid to come out, afraid of Dad's yelling and swinging arms, but ever-ready to step forward and plead, no, Daddy don't go! We love you!

But divorce? Never.

Dee-dee wiped her tears. "Finished, Cat?"

Before I could say no (I could've used more Cap'n Crunch) she grabbed my wrist and tugged me to the front door.

On our way down we passed Robbie. He was still staring at the TV with his face turned away, so I couldn't tell if he was crying. Divorce explained Robbie's tears, those moments in school when his nose reddened, his eyes pinked, and silent tears rolled down his cheeks. As Robbie cried, kids kept eating, laughing, and climbing the monkey bars. At first he'd gotten teased for being such a crybaby, but since he cried quietly every day, kids soon ignored him. His crying became invisible.

But not to me. Every day in Mr. Swanson's room I'd wanted to reach across my desk, touch Robbie's shoulder and ask, why are you crying? Or, what's the matter Robbie? Or, stop crying Robbie! Crying makes it worse. Crying seals your fate. Nobody likes a boy who cries. Please stop crying Robbie. But I said nothing at school, nothing at recess, and nothing that day at Dee-dee's.

Dee-dee wrapped in her orange hippie shawl and I followed her out into the cold afternoon. We were headed for my house. Bossy Holly would be gone by then.

We passed the Andersons out digging, the bratty twins tossing a ball, and Mrs. Zupinski biking by with her red smile, her basket of flyers, and her big rear end swallowing the bike seat. Mrs. Zupinski gave us a happy ring-ring as Dee-dee and I slipped between houses, past our towering birdhouse and down to the lake.

On our little strip of sand we listened to the sounds of the ice dismantling. The wind turned Dee-dee's hair into dancing snakes. Goosebumps rose on my arms. Crows gathered in the Andersons' cottonwoods. I picked up a rock and sent it skidding across frozen Little Rose Lake. I took up another rock and skidded it across. I stood apart from Dee-dee, squinted at the ice, took up rocks, and skidded them across.

I didn't do what I wanted to do.

I didn't stand close to Dee-dee, pick up her wrists, make her arms encircle me and sink into her patchouli warmth. Instead I threw rocks.

"Read it out loud, Cat."

"What?"

"The note."

Another crow landed as I unfolded the yellowed note, tender in my hands, and squinted at the wavery cursive.

"Deare Yee Who finde this. Heed Me with all yore Hearte I sorely hope & pray. Fore I have the Blood Sickness in Mee & will surely die afore Sunrise."

I shivered. The wind stabbed my eyes, my hands were red-cold, the ice tinkled and sighed. I wanted to be up sitting by a crackling fire, not down here with the creaking ice.

"Aren't you cold, Dee-dee?"

"Go on, Cat."

I kicked at a frozen stone and read on.

"I beg Yee carry out My Lasst Wish. Allow Nott My Dotter Tess to marry the Black-Hearted Blacksmythe Broaderick Blevvins. For He be God's Curse Uppon Earth. & allow nott Tess to Marry the Scrawnee Tinker Halvors Halvorrson. For though he have hidden Gold thair be no Fire betwixt them."

"No fire," muttered Dee-dee, nodding me on.

"Instead I beg Yee press Tess hard & fast into Wedlock with the Boy Who Haulls in the Mush."

"The boy who hauls in the mush?"

"That's what it says. The Boy Who Haulls in the Mush."

Dee-dee wiped her nose.

"Read the rest."

"That's all."

"Is there not a name? Or a date?"

I shook my head. Both the upper right hand corner and the lower left had been torn away.

Dee-dee adjusted her shawl. "Let us go for a walk, Cat."

I carefully slid the note back into my pocket and we set off for the far side of Little Rose, followed by the crows. We passed Andersons' fire pit, dock, and the tall cottonwoods where Mr. Anderson nailed the heads of his Northern Pike catches to the trees.

Those dried fish heads smiled down at us with their hundreds of tiny sharp teeth as we balanced on narrow strips of sand, broke white sheets of ice, skipped over melting puddles and climbed what was left of the crystallized snowbanks. We risked falling in, risked getting wet, and risked mangling our shoes as we edged along the chain link fence of the house beyond.

I did mangle my shoes. The metal fence tore gashes in the fake leather, then we ran out of houses and hit the tangle of young woods. Dee-dee and I crouched, crawled and picked our way through the saplings, thorny bushes and willows, catching seeds and stickers in our clothes and hair.

At the freeway wall where the storm sewer gaped, Dee-dee watched as I climbed its cold cement roundness, got on my belly, let my arms dangle and shouted into the black mouth with my voice reverberating.

"Hello in there! Hell-ell-ell oh-oh-oh in there-ere-ere!"

I thought it was funny.

Dee-dee didn't laugh.

We kept walking beyond the storm sewer, past our frowning church. Nearly hidden in tangled undergrowth was the old stone foundation of the long-ago ice house, now just a low stone wall of rocks round as skulls.

We sat on the moss-covered wall, feeling the smooth and rough surfaces of stone and mortar, scratching up moss in our fingernails and staring at the houses across the lake, Greens', Andersons', our McCloud house, Carters', Blakes', Zupinskis', Stringbean's—all the patios and yards empty now, no barbeques, lawnmowers, or inner tubes—just dwindling snow, brown grass, and yellow-gray ice.

Dee-dee drew a twisted joint from under her shawl and pointed at the freeway wall towards Big Snake Lake.

"Thousands of animals died over there, Cat. Those shores are soaked in blood. And not just pigs and cows."

I shrugged.

Our whole neighborhood used to be a hog farm. We kids still found rusty bits of barbed wire down by the lake, the ice house we sat upon was once a storehouse for the slaughtered meat from the Big Snake Lake Stockyards, and every summer White Rock celebrated Stockyard Days to commemorate all that long-ago killing.

Dee-dee passed the joint to me.

I held it between my fingers.

It was too dangerous to let any smoke in my lungs or the trees would start whispering. Sitting on that wall made my butt cold, and in my back pocket, along with that delicate yellowed note, was the crumbling dust of my latest failed perfection.

I should have stood up in that moment. If I knew what was coming I would have stood up. I could have passed the joint back to Dee-dee, slid off that wall, walked home and picked up my exacto knife. I should have never spoken to Dee-dee Morton again, never let her in my room, and never slept in her bed.

If I'd just kept carving away—

Then nobody would be dead.

The houses across the lake faded into a blur as I recalled the endless winter before I met Dee-dee.

That fall, Mom had stood in the kitchen chopping a green pepper. I had sat at the dining room table swamped by adolescence. My head was heavy in my hands, my arms heavy, my legs heavy, my whole body so heavy with the weight of my unlived life I could hardly breathe. Mom stepped from the kitchen and set something at my elbow. Tink. A fresh box of chalk. I couldn't turn my head, but I heard the *tink* a stick of chalk makes when clinking up against other sticks in a box. What is that for? I thought. Mom said why don't you carve a chalk canoe? *Carve a chalk canoe?* I'd never heard of such a thing. I didn't ask, carve a chalk canoe with what? I was already friends with the exacto knife I used to shape infinitesimal Playdoh hot dogs for my Barbie doll houses. But the exacto knife was in the art supply drawer, too far to reach. Mom walked to the drawer, rustled through, and set the exacto knife by me. Sharp. It was sharp. I drew out a stick of chalk. PERFECT. *It was perfect.* Not a mar on it. No rising pimples, aching buds, or stench of adolescence. It was smooth in my hands, smooth on my nose, and smooth on my cheek, and eleven other perfect sticks waited in that box. Mom said, I find it's easiest to get started by making one score lengthwise along the shaft. I know what a canoe looks like, I thought. I made one score lengthwise along the shaft. Mom said, it's best to carve out carefully from each side of the score to create the hollow in which the paddler will sit. I know what I'm doing! I said, and began carving carefully along the score. Mom said, before the insides become too hollow, and therefore too delicate, I find it's best to start on the end points. I know! I hissed, and started on the end points. Scritch-scratch as Dad's ballgame played in the living room, scritch-scratch as Mom assembled our upcoming supper, scritch-scratch the canoe revealed itself as white powder fell to my lap. When my hand slipped and the blade pierced my skin, drawing a bead of blood, I went on carving. Then snap, the canoe broke in my hands. Too thin, I thought, and vowed to try another. Mom kept quiet as I pulled out a new stick and began again. Insides, outsides, scritch-scratch, one stick after another, I scraped away for hours on hours, then days on days, hunched over, exerting my will. Twelve sticks in a box times one hundred boxes from Red Owl and Mini Mart and life passed by outside our dining room window as I sat inside endlessly carving. Falling leaves, Halloween, Thanksgiving, Christmas Eve, the canoes broke in my hands, the blade slipped, tiny cuts opened. While all the other kids were out skating and sledding, I was inside trying to carve a perfect chalk canoe. A pile of brokens rose in the dining room. Chalk dust filled the air, I was a chalk ghost, and no matter how carefully I carved, they always broke. Cracked in half. In my hands. On the verge of perfection. But I never gave up trying to carve a perfect chalk canoe.

Then came Dee-dee Morton.

And I set down my exacto knife.

I handed the smoking joint back to Dee-dee.

She took a last suck, tucked the remains under her shawl, and slid off the old stone foundation.

I followed, shivering cold. We picked our way through the woods at the lake-edge, crouching and crawling through more saplings and willows. Near Bullfrog Creek we spied creatures frozen under, perfectly preserved, a minnow, a crayfish, a bullhead.

Further on, where the water flowed close, we saw living things. A perch flicked, a sunny darted, a frog dashed, its spots circled in gold.

Things were coming alive under the ice!

We began to edge out, following the creatures that had survived winter.

Bullfrog Creek connected Little Rose Lake to Big Snake Lake through a low culvert, and the closer we got to the creek-mouth, the more creatures we saw under, alive and moving, sunnies, a perch, a crayfish. A snapping turtle—

A big one! Maybe Old Joe!

No, not big enough. Old Joe was as big as a hula hoop.

That's what my brothers and sisters used to say, Old Joe is this big, as their arms went wide.

Watch out for Old Joe.

Mr. Anderson once caught a huge snapper and let it walk around on the patch of concrete under his oak, tapping its nose with a stick to keep it from wandering. That snapper bit the stick as we kids gathered. Don't come too close, Mr. Anderson warned, or he'll snap off a finger. Is that Old Joe? we asked. No, Mr. Anderson said, this here isn't Old Joe. Old Joe is much bigger. This here is likely Old Joe's son. Or daughter? Mr. Anderson nodded. What are you gonna do with her? Mr. Anderson grinned his thin curl of a grin and said *make turtle soup.*

No turtles Dee-dee and I saw that day were Old Joe, none big enough, and entranced by the creatures we saw under, we further dared the ice. As the ice grew blacker, we tried to make ourselves lighter.

Shuffling carefully, we edged nearly to Bullfrog Creek, where the Chippewa once grew wild rice and wild battles raged.

Where the ice got too thin I went in.

To my knees—

Then my hands—

I gasped. My heart fought to escape my ribcage.

Dee-dee went to her stomach and reached for my wrists. She got hold of one wrist, then the other, and pulled and pulled.

Ice broke under my belly, hurt my skin, and froze me cold.

Finally Dee-dee slid me to the bank.

Boy was I cold. And wet. With a red scrape on my belly.

We had to walk back the long way, same way we came. We couldn't risk cutting across or walking the creek. On the way back my hands turned white, my feet went numb, and my teeth clacked, but I didn't faint, so Dee-dee didn't kiss me.

And before we took that walk towards the creek that ended so perilously, when we still sat on the ice house foundation, Dee-dee spidered her fingers into a crack in the old stone wall and drew out another yellowed note.

And everafter, I followed Dee-dee Morton and her spidering fingers, and at every turn when I should have said no, and could have said no, I said yes.

FIVE

"I, Broderick Blevvins, Evil Blacksmythe-"

Dee-dee was reading the second yellowed note aloud in my old four-poster. She'd run me a hot bath, made me chicken noodle soup and tucked me in to settle my shivers.

Now she was up close with her tickling hair and husky voice. As she read I began to nod off. The cold had exhausted me. So had the aftershock of her kiss (that wasn't a kiss). *The Bare Lips of One Girl Must Never Touch the Bare Lips of Another.*

That was the White Rock Rule. But I wondered if where Dee-dee came from it wasn't forbidden. Maybe big city girls could kiss each other all over. Maybe they could kiss each other on the lips and the neck and the breasts, then let their mouths go down to each other's waterfall of mystery.

Dee-dee's nearness filled my ears with cotton. As the words of the note floated from her mouth, I let one of my hands slowly migrate towards one of her ripe breasts. I was almost touching it through her green sweater. Then the back of my hand was barely on it. Then the back of my hand pressed against it.

Its heat, softness, and density surprised me.

My hand flipped and clutched her whole—

"Cat!"

Holly stood in my bedroom doorway with her arms crossed.

"What are you doing? Come help with supper! Dad'll be home soon. We have to clean up!"

I bolted from bed, headed for the rag drawer, in the mad dash to clean our house so DAD WOULD NOT GET MAD. On Fridays Mom worked late at the First State Bank of White Rock, so we girls had to clean up and make supper. With a dishtowel over my shoulder and a washrag in hand, I raced through the living room, emptying ashtrays, wiping TV trays, then to the bathroom, swiping tiles, polishing glass, then back to the kitchen to wash dishes as Holly stirred and chopped.

I forgot about Dee-dee. She still lingered, sniffing around our dining room, glancing into the living room, studying Mom's ecstatic quilts, my sister's sparkly dioramas, and my bloody pile of broken chalk canoes, then she stood in the bathroom staring into the mirror and touching her eyelashes. As I rolled the vacuum from the hall closet and began to uncoil the cord, Dee-dee wrapped up in her shawl and walked out the front door.

"See you later, Cat."

After making supper Holly left on her date. Dad and I ate in the living room watching All in the Family.

When the phone rang I answered in the kitchen.

"Hello, McClouds'."

A deep voice said, "Who is this?"

I swallowed. "This is Cat McCloud."

"Is your mother home?"

"No, she's not home. May I take a message?"

"Yes you may take a message. Tell your mother we are driving over there right now to kill her. Then we are gonna kill you, Cat McCloud. Then kill your sister. And your daddy too. We are on our way right now to kill all of you. We have guns and we are gonna blast you to pieces."

Click. Dial tone.

"Hello?"

We are on our way now to blast you to pieces.

I couldn't move. I sat in the high chair with the phone frozen to my face, the long cord dangling, and the words ringing.

Kill you, kill your mom, kill your daddy.

Don't Upset Your Father was the rule drilled into me since birth. DO NOT UPSET YOUR FATHER. But I figured this phone call overruled that. If killers were on their way to kill us right now, I should probably tell Dad.

I stepped into the canned laughter of the living room.

"Uh, Dad?"

"Yes, kiddo?"

He moved his eyes from the TV to me.

"Um, did you get enough to eat?"

"Yes I did kiddo."

He jiggled his ice, tapped his ash.

"Can I get you anything else?"

"No thank you."

"Uh, someone just called for Mom. They left a message."

I told Dad the message.

Dad called the police.

The cop on the other end said it was likely a prank call. Crank call, Stringbean and I called it. We'd done plenty of crank calls, but never this bad.

The cops said they'd send two officers over.

I locked the front door, which we never locked, then locked the door to the garage which we never locked, then went downstairs and locked the back door which we only locked against the window-peeper. Then I went to my room, turned off the lights, and peered through the blinds.

My window faced Little Rose Lake Road, the only approach for the killers if they were coming by car. Were they coming by car? Yes they'd said, we are driving there right now to kill you. They were coming by car. They were a car-full of killers on their way to kill us right now.

It was dark by then, and every car going by was a shark trolling the bottom of the ocean for us. Was it this car? Was it that? Who'd come first? The cops or the killers? As I watched from my darkened window my heart nearly tore from my ribs and up into the night.

Finally a car pulled into our driveway. Dark with a white stripe. The White Rock Police. We gathered in the dining room to answer their questions. Did Mom have any enemies? Any grudges against her? Any reason for anyone to threaten her? No, Dad said, Mom was kind to everybody. Everybody liked her. But there was that recent robbery at the First State Bank of White Rock. Mom was the only teller, Dad said, to press the silent alarm. As the teller on Mom's left was emptying her drawers, and the teller on Mom's right was on her knees praying sweet Jesus don't let them kill me, and the robbers were warning, don't press the alarm or we'll kill you, Mom was pressing the alarm.

What Dad didn't tell the cops was that after Mom pressed the alarm, she ran out after the robbers to see if she could get a look at their faces or their license plate. That was Mom, unafraid of armed robbers, a houseful of teenagers, or an oncoming tornado. During tornados she'd climb to our roof to watch the show, but crank or not, we found the means of that threatening phone call in the *White Rock Reader*, open on our dining room table.

LOCAL HEROINE

Mrs. Donald McCloud (Edith), 50, wife of Mr. Donald (Don) McCloud, 53, 1959 Little Rose Lake Road, mother of ten, with Holly, 17, and Catherine (Cat), 13, still residing at home, was awarded a Medal of Bravery for her part in the capture of three robbers at the First State Bank of...

There it was. Our names and address. Anybody could look in the White Rock Directory for our phone number. Either it was a crank, or a compadre of the robbers, but whoever it was, when Mom came home she wasn't alarmed. "Oh that was just a prank call," she said as she dug into supper then headed downstairs to sew.

Dad sat up late in his olive green lazy-boy waiting for Holly to come home from her date. I went to bed, but couldn't eat my usual two bowls of Blue Bunny vanilla ice cream sprinkled with Tang, Breakfast Drink for Astronauts (with enough spit stirred in to make it creamy). Instead I pulled from under my pillow the damp and wrinkled softness Dee-dee had drawn from the cracks of the old stone foundation and read yellowed note number two.

I, Broderick Blevvins, Evile Blacksmithe, dew laff! Ha-ha! Me wikkid laffter rings in mee Blacksmythe Shoppe! Me laffter rings with mee Irons & mee Tonngs! It crakles with mee Fyre & Grones with thee Whind on this Goddforesakyne Prayree! Butt oh! Wun daye I shall rule this Damned Prayree! Aye! & mee sire shall Rule too! For the nixt lass I dew Marry shall be Tess of the dying Fotther. & whin Tess dew bye mee be bedded, & whin She dew bye mee growe with Chylde & whin She dew deelliver mee a Sonn, thin shall I kipp her brace-letted weth Irons, yea, kipp her Prisoned till me Boye bee wheaned & thin shall Tess bee killt by my Hand & baried with all thim uther Lasses whoos Bones rest beehynde mee Evile Blacksmythe Shoppe! Ha-ha!

Baried with all thim uther Lasses? Now I really couldn't sleep. To soothe (distract) myself, I slid from its hiding place the Tom Robbins paperback I'd snuck (borrowed) (stolen) from my big brother, and from which I read only the juicy parts. After finding a few references to bare breasts, the heat in my hips came alive and my fingers worked down to my waterfall of mystery. Then I fell asleep and dreamed of bank robbers creeping through our house, while in the basement the blacksmith hammered out his evil plans. Tong-tong!

SIX

When the phone rang the next morning Mom picked it up.

On Saturdays Mom drove me crazy by vacuuming while I was still asleep. When she finally turned off the vacuum RING-RING went the telephone.

It might have been ringing the whole time she vacuumed. It might be the killers calling back to say they were coming right now. Something had delayed them last night, but now they were on their way to kill us and soon we'd be a diorama of a slaughtered family, Holly sprawled in her baby-doll nightie, Dad face-down in his coffee, Mom slumped by the running vacuum, and me in my bloody four-poster with the dirty paperback.

Instead it was Stringbean saying let's bike to Sunnyvale Shopping Senter. That's how it was spelled. *SHOPPING SENTER.* Stringbean was plotting to leave chewed-up blobs of Hubba Bubba Bubble Gum on the floor of Sunnyvale so we could watch shoppers step on them then lift their shoes in disgust as we silently cracked up.

Stringbean's hands were the size of dinner plates and she wore her hair in two long blond braids, then one day she snipped off her braids so her hair was as short as the neighbor boys' she was always running off with.

Stringbean ran with the boys, fished with the boys, and shot baskets with them, but when she turned thirteen and it came

time for her to turn into a lady, her mom started buying her
fluffy sweaters from the covers of Seventeen Magazine and
leaving cute flowered barrettes in the bathroom, and her dad
began suggesting she stop playing ball with the boys, and the
boys said you can't play with us anymore, Stringbean.

Stringbean's best pals shut the door on her but the Ladyhood
door stayed shut too. Her breasts didn't grow, her pubic hair
didn't sprout, and her private parts didn't bleed. Stringbean was
stuck between girlhood and boyhood, six feet tall and ANGRY.

Her bike was a ten-speed and she rode it expertly, with no
fear. I was wobbly on my old Schwinn as I biked to her house.
There she stuffed her knapsack full of Hubba Bubba Bubble
Gum, sticks long as my forearm and thick as my finger, then we
set off for Silver Trout Road. I had to ride beside Stringbean.
This wasn't safe. She'd purposely veer into me, drive me to the
curb, then bike ahead laughing.

When we finally got to Sunnyvale we planted ourselves by
the shallow pool in the open square and chewed as we watched
shoppers. We saw the lunch lady (hardly recognizable without
her hairnet) and Mrs. Zupinski (with her red smile and big butt).
Then we spied bossy Holly with Stringbean's sassy sister Melody,
and ducked behind the pool, out of sight.

Shoppers' voices bounced off the shiny floor, water burbled
in the aquamarine pool, and we chewed and chewed Hubba
Bubba till our jaws turned to rock. We swallowed the first gouts
of juicy sweetness and chewed on till the gum was bland and
stiff, then changed our ways.

"It's better," Stringbean discovered, "to chew only a little bit,
so it's still soft and sticky, so when they step on it, it really
sticks."

This was true. The more sugary our wads, the more sticky,
but being from a less prosperous home, I was reluctant to waste
any of the juicy sweetness.

Stringbean had to coach me, her long fingers close to my
mouth, as a lady in red platforms approached.

"Take it out! Take it out!"

I pushed the gum out with my tongue.

Stringbean took it in her fingers.

She found the perfect moment. She had the knack. She got in front of the platform lady, placed the gum, and stepped away. Did the platform lady not see? She stepped right on the Hubba Bubba! Her platform stuck to the floor. She fought to unstick it, lifted her shoe to inspect and almost fell over! HA-HA! We silently cracked up. So much fun shopping with Stringbean!

It was worth the treacherous ride home.

On the way back Stringbean bumped into Mrs. Zupinski with her basket full of flyers. Mrs. Zupinski's bike wobbled and tipped and all her flyers went flying along Silver Trout Road. We helped her gather the flyers and stack them back in her basket and she smiled her big red smile, but I could tell deep inside Mrs. Zupinski was red-hot mad.

When I got home, Dee-dee was sitting on my front steps with her face completely curtained by blond locks.

She parted her locks, revealing pink-rimmed eyes.

"My dad moved out," she sniffed.

I planted my kickstand and sat down beside her.

I smelled the softening earth, the damp leaves in the crack, and Dee-dee's patchouli, faint with tangerine.

Would this be a moment, I wondered, when one girl could put her arm around another?

She could lean on me, her tears would drip, her body would sigh, the steps would drop away, the house would fall behind, and I would rise in endless ecstasy.

Better not risk it.

I knew what they did to bad girls—

I knew since a wee girl.

Long ago Dad took me to the hardware store out on Old Highway Eight where the weeds grew up through the cracks in the road. From that hardware store, Dad took home many narrow boxes, and in our basement bathroom, from those boxes Dad drew out plastic tiles the suntan shade of Cover Girl Liquid Makeup embedded with swirls of brunette hair. Those swirls of hair belonged to the Brunette Breck Girl. Once one of the perfect young ladies on the back of Ladies Home Journals advertising Breck Shampoo with her perfect face, perfect hair and perfect behavior, the Brunette Breck Girl went bad. She went bad by following her heart. She danced wild at the Blue Moon Ballroom, and she sweated in a golden mini-dress. Then she went to the Ladies' Room to cool off and refresh, and while there she kissed boys, and kissed girls, and did all kinds of lovely things to them that gave them all great pleasure. This made her very bad. So they took her to the factory on Old Highway Eight where the weeds grew up through the cracks in the road and skinny ladies in hairnets said, come here dear, this won't hurt, this will be just like a girl-size car wash. Take off all your clothes and step up on this metal grate. The girl took off her clothes and stepped up on the metal grate. Down over her came a big glass jar. And at first it was just like a girl-size car wash. Soap and water foamed up and washed the bad girl clean. Then up from the bottom came the giant Osterizer blender blades. First they stirred the girl, then they pureed her, then liquefied her, and all her juices went running down the drain and were pumped to different parts of the factory where they were mixed with plastics and turned into Barbie dolls, and Tupperware, and hula hoops. But the hair did not dissolve. It got caught in the grate. So the skinny ladies gathered it up and pressed it into hairy bathroom tiles. There were brunette tiles, blond tiles, even gray tiles from the bad old ladies.

That is what they did to girls who were bad in White Rock.

And there I was—

Smelling the damp earth and the patchouli, and about to put my arm around Dee-dee Morton.

Dee-dee squinted at the clouds above the houses.

I squinted at the clouds. The sun behind was slowly sinking.

Dee-dee leaned back on her elbows. I leaned back on mine.

She closed her eyes. I closed mine.

Her pinky finger slid towards me.

The tips of our pinkies touched—

A river of electricity ran between us.

Through my closed lids the sun broke, and for the first time that year, I felt the sun's heat through my jeans. My stomach was sour from all the Hubba Bubba I'd swallowed back at Sunnyvale, but below the sourness something turned sweet. Perhaps spring would finally come to White Rock. Perhaps our tulips would push up, and Andersons' apple trees would bloom, and all the leaves on Little Rose Lake would unfurl in an embarrassment of green.

And perhaps the moist May air would soften that dried-up mummy on Dee-dee's bed.

Perhaps in June, the hardened thing would flower with mold.

And what was Dee-dee going to do with the mummy in July's high humidity?

And where did she get that mummy in the first place?

"We are meditating, Cat."

I peeked through my closed lids.

Dee-dee was now sitting cross-legged.

"We are letting our sodden thoughts float up to the sky. We are releasing the worries of this life and letting in the infinite. Do not open your eyes, Cat. Just breathe."

I squirmed.

"And do not move. Do not move even if an insect crawls on you. Just let it crawl. Let it crawl and feel everything."

There wasn't an insect on me but I did have to pee.

"Feel the fullness and breathe."

The breeze took up a strand of her hair, teasing my arm.

"You are entering a deeper part of yourself. You are descending into your belly. You are entering the space above your naval."

I was entering the space wherein sat huge chunks of Hubba Bubba.

"Go deeper."

I was entering my full bladder.

"And deeper."

I was entering the place that burned for girls and boys, the place hot with passion for fainting, kissing, and imagining, the dark heat that drove me.

"And deeper."

I was entering the place where my rear end touched our cold cement steps. If we sat there much longer my pee would seep out, drip into the crack and wake the creatures sleeping there. They'd smell my teenage piss and hatch a plan.

"Feel yourself dissolve into the blah…

"Feel yourself become one with the blah…

"Feel yourself entering the blah…

As Dee-dee's voice went on, I didn't care if they put me in the blender and I got trapped forever in some bathroom tiles, not if I could feel Dee-dee's flowing river of electricity.

"Cat, what are you doing?"

Holly's boom interrupted our oncoming oneness. Holly stood at the foot of our steps with a J. C. Penney's bag.

"Why are you just sitting there? You should be painting the garage. It's warm enough. You told Dad you'd do it."

Holly had bought herself something at Sunnyvale. Holly could afford new clothes because she worked. Holly worked and cleaned and contributed to the household, and I was a good-for-nothing who did nothing all day but daydream and suffer. And I'd told Dad I'd paint the garage.

I glanced at Dee-dee, her fingers now in flower shapes.

Holly rolled her eyes and stepped around.

I sighed and got up.

As I lifted the garage door, and dragged out the ladder, and climbed with the tools and rags, Dee-dee still sat meditating. Dad came out and showed me the right way to scrape (short jabby strokes) and the proper way to paint (long sweeping strokes) and as I painted, ants got caught in the paint, trapped in stickiness, such a short life, just hatched into spring then BAM dead.

Death was everywhere that day. Death in Holly's frown, death in the dying ants, and death in my dead brain as I painted knowing my life was over and I'd always be a nothing slaving away at endless garage doors while Dee-dee sat meditating on our steps, all lovely and untouchable.

Mom popped her head out the front door.

"Cat, did you get in the mail yesterday?"

The mail, the mail. Yes I did get the mail. The Red Owl flyer, the Minnegasco bill, and that unstamped letter to Tammy (who didn't live here anymore, but did bring cute boys down to the lake, cute boys with long hair and beards and sandals like Jesus).

Where had I put that mail? I'd been walking home from school, then Dee-dee put her fingers in the crack, then Holly came and we ran and what did I do with the letters? Did I take them to Dee-dee's? Don't think so. Where did I leave them? By the tulip bed?

I glanced down. No letters. Perhaps the wind had taken them. I descended the ladder and looked around.

Dee-dee opened her eyes, reached under her hippie shawl, and drew out the Red Owl flyer, the Minnegasco bill, and the letter to Tammy.

"We have to talk, Cat."

She gestured for me to come close and whispered.

"A Poison Pen lives in this neighborhood."

"A what?"

"Someone who dips their pen in venom to hurt others."

A Poison Pen? In our neighborhood?

"Give your mother these." Dee-dee handed me the gas bill and the Red Owl flyer. "But do not give your sister this." She wagged the Tammy letter. "We cannot open this here, Cat. We cannot let this poison out anywhere near your house."

She stood, flicking her hair. "Follow me."

I followed her up past Highlook Drive to the meadow with the haunted Ford truck. That truck had sat surrounded by weeds ever since White Rock was a hog farm. Once upon a time the Ford was red and green, but time had crazed the paint into crackles and now it was mostly rust, with a spiderweb-crack in the windshield. We figured someone died in that truck, but so long ago their bloodstains blended with the rust. In there were crumpled cigarette packs and empty whisky bottles. Straw spilled out the seat springs. Mice made their beds in the stuffing, their little droppings scattered on the floor.

Dee-dee and I hunched in the busted seats. The air was full of floating things. She drew the envelope from under her shawl. Her fingers traced the flap-edge. She tapped out a typewritten page of translucent onionskin.

"I cannot say these words out loud, Cat."

She passed the letter to me.

"You should not speak them out loud either."

I read silently.

Dear Tammy McCloud,

You are a WHORE. I have seen your whorish ways.
I have seen the paltry scraps of fabric with which you
barely cover your nakedness. I have seen the leering
young men you bring to the lake to seduce with your
whorish ways. I have seen their long hair, uncut
beards and ragged cutoffs. I have seen their hippie
sandals. I have seen you not only smoking cigarettes.
I have seen you smoking evil weed and drinking
alcohol. In your drunkenness you throw sand at each
other. God knows what else you do with those hippie
boys underwater.

Tammy McCloud I warn you. STAY AWAY from
my boys. And burn that bikini! Put on a decent one-
piece. They are for sale at J. C. Penney's and
Montgomery Wards. If you can afford two little
scraps of fabric, then you can afford a J. C. Penney
one-piece. Cover your NAKEDNESS!

Sincerely,
A Concerned Neighbor

Who'd write such a letter? Dee-dee and I sat in that old Ford
investigating the envelope, the typeface, and the angry words.
We held the letter to the sun, sniffed it, and studied it with our
naked eyes, then took it back to her dad's study (filled with fat
books of ancient Egypt and unearthed curiosities).

There we held the Poison Pen under a magnifying glass and
inspected the onionskin. Were there fingerprints? None we could
see. Were there smudges? Or tell-tale stains? None visible. Was
there a unique flaw in the typeface? Yes! The lower case g had a
missing tail. But who'd delivered it? With no stamp or return
address, someone must have walked up, opened our mailbox and
stuck it in. Someone on our street. *A concerned neighbor.*

"A neighbor with boys," Dee-dee said. "Somebody whose
windows face the lake. Someone on your side who can look out
and watch Tammy go down to swim."

That ruled out the bratty twins and Laura, Laurel, and Lori. On our side all the neighbors' picture windows faced the lake. But who had boys? The Andersons' boys were grown and moved away. The Carters had three boys, my age and younger. The Zupinskis had two boys my age and younger. The Blakes had boys and girls of all ages.

"Binoculars," Dee-dee said, leading me back to her room. "That is how they see your sister. We will need to scope out the sightlines. And stake out your mailbox."

She bent over her cigar box, describing how we'd lie in wait, hidden in my uncle's Chevy Blazer to catch the letter-writer red-handed, but I wasn't interested in lying belly-down in that stinky old Blazer, and I didn't care who saw Tammy in her bikini. We girls all wore bikinis. Some of us just wore them more protuberantly than others. *Protuberantly, robustly, curvaceously.* There were many adjectives to describe my big sisters in their bikinis.

My bikini wasn't protuberant. I couldn't help that. Tammy's bikini was protuberant and she couldn't help that. But Tammy wasn't a whore. Filling out your swimsuit didn't make you a whore. Tammy laughed with the boys, but didn't let them kiss her. And what if she did? What was a whore anyway? A girl who laughed with boys and let them kiss her? What was the big deal?

Dee-dee went on about wayward women, women called *sluts* and *heathens*, and how the religions of the world used their rules throughout history to control women, keep them down, and how the church called wise women *witches* and burned them at the stake. "Burned them alive," she whispered. "By the thousands. And people still do it, to themselves, when they want to protest something. Like this Buddhist monk."

She opened a Life magazine to a black-and-white photo of a monk burning in the street, his eyes closed as if in perfect peace. "It is called IMMOLATION, Cat. And it might look," she read my mind, "as if he is in perfect peace. But his skin is not at peace. It hurts like HELL. I read it in a book on suicide. Some people burn themselves instead of taking pills or jumping off a cliff, and it is a big mistake." Dee-dee opened a black book to a somber woman covered in scars. "This woman thought she had nothing to live for, so she poured gasoline over herself, struck a match, and lived to tell. She said it hurt like hell. The worst pain ever."

The worst pain ever.

I wasn't listening. My eyes were on the mummy beside us, silent and still. Was he dreaming of hot deserts and the cool Nile? Or was his spirit off in the Underworld with the animal-headed gods and goddesses?

I'd long ago fallen in love with the Science Museum of Minnesota mummy. It rested alone in a glass case in its own dark room, lit only by dioramas of pyramid-building, tiny figures hauling rope and dragging stones. I'd wander alone to that room and stand over that mummy in wordless worship. I felt a strange kinship, a buzz of familiarity.

Perhaps the mummy on Dee-dee's bed was one and the same. Had Dee-dee stolen the Science Museum mummy? Had she hauled it out at midnight? Her dad was an Egyptologist. Perhaps she had access, behind the scenes?

No, I deduced as the furry Persian purred on me. That mummy on Dee-dee's bed wasn't from the Science Museum. The Science Museum mummy had a different mouth, and three missing toes, and its loins were girded in swaddling cloth. This mummy had all its toes, and while clearly male, with that bit of beef jerky between its legs, it was bare-hipped.

Dee-dee went on about "the demonization of femininity" as I recalled when Mom drove me to Chicago to see the Treasures of Tutankhamun. The deeper we walked through the exhibit, the more exquisite were the objects, the finer the handiwork. How did they make those intricacies of gold and lapis lazuli? How did they master such infinitesimal perfection? And wasn't there a curse attached to the finders, to Carter and his diggers? Hadn't they all died mysteriously after opening the tomb? Weren't they cursed for disturbing the resting place of a mummy?

I dared touch the mummy's arm. It was hard as petrified wood, and slippery, as if glazed.

"We've got to get this back to wherever it came from," I said.

Dee-dee raised a warning palm. Her eyes went dull. She lowered her chin and circled her hands.

"I am going to put you under now, Cat. I am going to cast

you into a trance. I am going to send you deeply—"

My stomach gave the curlicue sound: hungry.

"I have to go."

Dee-dee didn't try to stop me. As I walked home I pondered. Every time I broached the subject of where that mummy came from, Dee-dee circled her hands, chanted deeply, and tried to put me under. What would she do, I wondered, if I came right out and asked, *where did that mummy come from?*

Next morning I woke from a nightmare of Dee-dee burning at the stake, all her beautiful skin blistering. *Immolation,* she'd whispered the day before, they burned the women called witches, *burned them alive.* How could they do it, I wondered. How could they bind the ropes and stack the wood then light the match? I had trouble killing an ant. How could they kill another human being? Did they use some kind of accelerant back then, lamp oil or animal fat, then stand back and watch the show? I couldn't burn, drown, or cut to pieces. Plenty of times I'd wanted to kill bossy Holly and sassy Melody and the bratty twins. I'd tried to kill them in my dreams. I'd squeeze their throats and watch their eyes bulge and it felt so good, but even in dreams I couldn't kill. I always woke first. And I'd wanted to kill myself for throwing the burger bag out the bus window on my sixth grade field trip when the bus filled with susurrations of *litterbug, litterbug.* But to kill another person? That would hurt like hell. *The worst pain ever.* That's what Dee-dee was feeling in my dream. The worst pain ever. But she wasn't screaming. Her face was peaceful, like the monk's in that Life magazine, and there was a crowd of townspeople below chuckling, smiling, their placid grins lit by the flames consuming Dee-dee. There were Mr. and Mrs. Anderson, the Blakes and their kids, bossy Holly and sassy Melody, Mr. and Mrs. Zupinski with Zipper and Flipper, the bratty twins, the Carters, and Mrs. Green with her yipping poodle, all chatting—hi, how are you, how's your family, fine, fine—as the wind took the flames and turned Dee-dee into a crusty black mummy.

SEVEN

Then spring came, ZING! The ice went out, our tulips pushed up, the crabapples flaunted their whorish beauty, and more yellowed letters emerged from the cracks of White Rock.

Under the haunted Ford truck Dee-dee found a letter from Tess to the Boy Who Hauled in the Mush.

> Deare Mush Boye, please bye Yore leaf do visitt
> Mee whin the Moon bee past the Orechard Whall.

In Andersons' oak was a love-note from Mush Boy.

> Deerist Tess, Eye dew spye Yee 'mongst the
> Flouwers & Eye dew yearne hartilee fore Yee, my
> heart yearneth nite and daye fore to holde Yee in
> mee arms till Yee burst.

By the storm sewer we found an evil Blacksmith scrawling.

> Bye Mee Evill Ways I shall dew all the Evill I kann
> Muster! With Mee Hammer! And Mee Tongs!

Then summer came, BAM! with its heat, sweat, and sparkle, roaring boats, humming lawnmowers, and raucous water-play. My sisters emerged in their fulsome bikinis, and I put every possible inch of my skin out in the sun and watched for every possible opportunity to put my arm around Dee-dee.

But very few moments presented themselves. Instead of becoming more maudlin at her parents' upcoming divorce, Dee-dee got REALLY PISSED OFF, casting spells this way and that, upon whatever displeased her, her weepy brother Robbie, the muggy weather, the cashier up at the Mini-Mart who wouldn't sell her Zig-Zag papers.

As Dee-dee and I uncovered more yellowed notes from the cracks of White Rock, we became as interested in the lives of the letter writers as my sister Tammy was in her soap operas. Would Tess marry the evil Blacksmith? Or run off with the Boy Who Hauled in the Mush? Or would she wed the well-off but boring Tinker? Though Tess's bones were long buried, no matter who she ended up marrying, we felt it was our duty to save her, by preventing her from wedding the Evil Blacksmith.

To do this we had to turn back Time. To find the perfect time-traveling spell we consulted Dee-dee's magic books. She had stacks in her bedroom, yellowed, leather-bound, falling-apart tomes full of spells for invisibility, spells for taking flight, spells for turning your enemies green with the bloated plague, and spells for turning back time. There were time-turning spells with powdered rhino horn, fermented dog tail, and pulverized cat intestines. There were spells calling for the bile of a murderer, the tongue of a liar, and the still-beating heart of a saint. And there were spells with seven days of fasting followed by seven days of feasting and seven nights of dancing upon graves. Then we found this:

> Gather two Drams Honey. Mash with pinch of Marigold. Leave in Light of Full Moon. Add two Dewdrops from Red Rose. Strain in Virgin's Hanky. Put under Tongue. Count One Hundred. Add One Wasp Stinger & Strap of Pigg. Spin Thrice.

That spell was our favorite. The ingredients were easy, some tasted good (we figured *strap of pigg* was bacon) and no cats nor dogs need suffer. But what time were we aiming for?

To find the answer we consulted the White Rock Library. We split the stack of history books in two and shared our newly-begotten knowledge while sun tanning down at the lake. I ran in and out of the water in my flat-chested bikini, as Mrs. Zupinski spied on us with her binoculars to her picture window, and Dee-dee stayed mostly on her towel. Dee-dee did a lot of reading and not much swimming.

Unlike Stringbean.

Stringbean and I used to spend all day in the lake. In the morning Stringbean would kick out her inner tube, we'd meet in the middle, and with our skin roasting we'd balance on the hot rubber, fall screaming into the lake, touch bottom and come up with a handful of muck. TOUCHED BOTTOM! How deep could we go? Some places were too deep and we never reached bottom before our ears screamed and lungs almost burst. And we'd have underwater breathing contests, Stringbean and I. Stringbean was never a mermaid (too sissy), but I'd hover underwater with my ankles crossed in a tailfin and use my mermaid powers to draw oxygen from the water through the pores of my skin. Then we'd swim to the shallows and force a leg in a muck hole shouting HELP! STUCK IN QUICKSAND!

But I didn't spend much time with Stringbean that summer. I was too busy preparing for time travel with Dee-dee. And Dee-dee wasn't much of a swimmer. After a lackluster dogpaddle to the raft and a few dives off, in which she nearly lost her bikini bottoms, Dee-dee returned to her towel and there she lay, pale skin dotted with water, ripe woman-breasts and wet woman-hair barely contained.

As she sat up to wring out her locks, water dripped from her elbows to her thighs, raising goosebumps.

Those sights and the cool lakewater made me salivate.

One hot afternoon Dee-dee propped herself up, drew a spiral notebook from her beach bag and paged through as I watched a water droplet head for her cleavage.

"Here is what I learned, Cat. The last recorded blacksmith in

White Rock was in 1908. You know what that means."

I shrugged.

"That means that we aim for no later than 1908. And the first white man set foot here in 1655."

She tilted her straw hat. "You know what that means."

I shrugged again. That sunhat hid her face.

Who under the age of forty wore a sunhat? No one but old Mrs. Anderson. Wise up, Dee-dee. We girls of White Rock wanted the sun on our faces. We wanted to be brown, like the girls in the movies and magazines. And I couldn't listen to any more history. Not with Dee-dee so up-close and wet. What would happen if I reached over and wiped up that water droplet before it disappeared in her cleavage?

A crow cawed from the Andersons' pines. Better not! A blue jay in our Russian olive warned, that's right! Or you'll be burned at the stake! Or drowned in the lake! Or worse yet, the tall cottonwoods sighed, worse than death by fire or water is if when you touch Dee-dee, she snarls LEZBO in disgust then runs up the hill never to be your friend again.

"So," Dee-dee was saying, "Our task is to turn back time to after Tess's father dies and before anybody marries her. Synchronize your watches."

I looked down at my empty wrist.

I hadn't been listening.

What had she said about blacksmiths and stockyards? Oh well, I could do my homework later, for as far as navigating long-ago White Rock, luckily for us, Mr. Harold B. Heggers had recently published a big red book with gold letters, STOCKYARD STORIES, the Rise of White Rock, complete with old pictures, maps, and drawings of once upon a time.

On those glossy pages were old silver plates of the White Rock Hotel where the stockyard men gathered to drink, play cards, and visit fancy ladies. There were tintypes of the killing pens and the railroad cars that took the meat to the city. There was the livestock huddled to be slaughtered. There was the tribe of Chippewa who for generations came to Bullfrog Creek to harvest wild rice. There were the farmers who raised the livestock and the butchers who cut it up, and there was the shore of Big Snake Lake where all the blood flowed. In those old sepia photos were faces with tough eyes, squinting eyes, sad eyes sunk in shadow. People back then had harder faces, polished by the winds, rubbed sharp and shiny like Mom's weathered driftwood. DON'T EFF WITH ME faces.

We should have listened to what those hollowed eyes were telling us. We should have listened to those hard faces. But we didn't listen, and we had no idea what we were getting into as we lay down at the lake covered in Coppertone with our stacks of history books, no idea what we were stirring up with our peeks into the past, and no idea what else was brewing that summer with the Poison Pen.

EIGHT

While Dee-dee and I planned our time travel adventures, her dad moved out. Mr. Morton took his old maps, brown bones, and hieroglyphics, and left a wastebasket full of crumpled research papers and a black Naugahyde couch in his study. We put the mummy on that couch so it could rest with a dehumidifier running day and night and not flower with mold.

That summer Robbie Morton had a kind of summer flowering. Robbie no longer sat in front of the TV with tears running down his cheeks. Robbie made friends with Zipper Zupinski. Zipper had the cutest grin, big and red like his mom's, and always curled up, as if he found every part of life amusing, even the painful, embarrassing parts, like when his swim trunks fell down, or he lost a fish, or slipped on the dock. Always that curl of a grin. Robbie and Zipper were always together that summer, splashing down at the lake, fishing off Zupinskis' dock, and putting up tents for sleepovers. No more tears alone in front of the TV for Robbie. They even, those rascals, tried to climb the thirty foot pole of our birdhouse.

One hot day Dee-dee tilted her sunhat and said, "Zipper, I bet you cannot climb that pole to the martin house." Zipper took any dare thrown at him. As Dee-dee, Robbie, Flipper, and I stood below craning our necks, wondering what he would find in the bird-holes, Zipper straddled that wooden pole and up he crept like a frog. He was halfway to the tiny house when we heard a CRACK! Zipper shimmied down fast, with me shaking my fist, "You made a crack in our birdhouse pole, Zipper Zupinski! Now you have to fix it!" But of course he never did. That crack stayed.

Meanwhile Dee-dee and I memorized our favorite time travel potion. In the dark of sleep-overs we'd recite it face-to-face, our noses almost touching. "Gather two drams Honey. Mash with pinch of Marigold. Leave in light of full Moon. Add dew from Red Rose. Strain in Virgin's Hanky. Put under Tongue. Count One Hundred. Add Wasp Stinger & Strap of Pigg. Spin Thrice!"

When the full moon of July finally came we were ready.

We doubled the potion, squeezed honey from a honey-bear, mashed in two pinches of marigold, and left the mixture on our patio in the light of the full moon.

Next morning the mixture was circled with ants. We debated whether or not to pick out the ants. Dee-dee said leave them in, dead ants help any potion. I said take them out, time travel is a delicate business. Dee-dee said okay if you pick them out.

Next we added two dewdrops from a rose (Mrs. Anderson's). We had to get up early, so Dee-dee slept over. No breast-touching this time. I didn't dare. Breast-touching was far too dangerous an undertaking for someone about to time travel.

We got up as the sun broke over Little Rose. The Great Blue Heron silently fished, the mist rose, and we crept into Mrs. Anderson's garden with an eyedropper. Getting a dewdrop from a rose isn't easy. Sometimes the dewdrop ran away. Sometimes it fell to the grass. Sometimes an ant nudged it, but I persisted, as Dee-dee breathed her hot breath on my cheek, watching me chase dew over the delicate folds of that velvety rose. I finally managed to suck up four drops.

We dripped the drops into the marigold mush and strained that through a virgin's hanky. Mine. (Dee-dee might be but I didn't ask.) Then we tied the hanky in our Russian olive tree as instructed. Frying two strips of bacon was easy. The wasp stingers were hard. How do you get the stinger of a wasp? First you have to find the nest. Then you have to kill a wasp. Then you have to pry out the stinger. Luckily we found one dead wasp in our garage and another on our living room windowsill. We lucked out, as Stringbean would say. But we couldn't dig out the stinger, so we took the whole wasps.

Before placing the strainings under our tongue, adding the bacon and wasps and spinning thrice, we had to prepare for going back in time. We had to prepare for the RIGHT time and for the WRONG time. We had to prepare for everything.

What if we got sent back to the time of the Chippewa? Or sucked back to our mothers' breasts? Or back to Prohibition in a shot-up gangster car? Or to the Ice Age? Or the inland sea? Or before the Big Bang when there was nothing? Or to the future where people lived crowded in flimsy plastic tubes to protect themselves from the environment they themselves poisoned?

All this we pondered that July.

"If we end up in the right time, what exactly will we do for Tess?" I asked one hot afternoon down at the lake.

"We are going to steal the Blacksmith's money and steal the Tinker's money, and give it to Tess, so she and Mush Boy have a trousseau," Dee-dee said.

A trousseau?

"No, Dee-dee, we're not stealing anything. True love can fend for itself. We're just going to make sure Tess doesn't marry the Evil Blacksmith. To save her life."

"But Cat," she gave me her flat look, "she is already dead."

"Dead now, but—"

"Dead either way," she smiled. "So, nothing to lose!"

The potion didn't specify time of use. It was to be prepared under the full moon, but after that the magic was up to us. We couldn't wait too long or the potion would sour, and we had to time travel before school started, in case there were glitches. We decided on midnight, July 29, during Stockyard Days, when all of White Rock celebrated its history of killing countless hooved creatures for meat.

There were fireworks and barbeques, the train station was strung with streamers, a band marched in a parade, and the old folks brought folding chairs.

I kept away except for the fireworks. Though set off on the

shores of Big Snake, they still gleamed over Little Rose.

The parade had taken place, the barbeques were sizzling, and the sunset smelled of burning flesh as Mom and Dad paddled our raft to the middle to watch the fireworks.

The mosquitoes were bad. Dee-dee and I watched from our beach with the bitter taste of Deep Forest OFF on our tongues.

We'd put up the blue tent. Dee-dee brought popcorn and pot. I brought hot dogs and the baggies of potion.

After Mom and Dad went up to the house, Dee-dee and I lit a fire, cut pointed sticks from Andersons' windfall branches, skewered hot dogs, and watched them spit and sizzle in the flames. As the fire flickered I told Dee-dee about the mayflies. If she thought the mosquitoes were bad, she should see the mayflies on the Mississippi, how they'd cluster by the millions.

"In late summer," I said, "they hatch, mate, and die, and their bodies get so thick on the bridges, they form a slippery paste and cause car accidents."

"Hatch, mate, and die," sighed Dee-dee.

"And when you swim through all those dead mayflies, you come up plastered in tiny corpses."

"Tiny corpses," Dee-dee said, cheeking her hot dog.

"And before they die, they fill the air like fairies with their long back-feelers open for mating on the wing."

"Fairies," chewed Dee-dee, "mating on the wing."

She'd never seen one. A mayfly I mean. Mayflies didn't venture inland to White Rock. But maybe one day Dee-dee would come boating with me on the Mississippi and we could sit on the bow in our bikinis and watch the river open before us as the engine roared and together we'd soar over the sparkling water, Dee-dee with her breasts bulging and golden locks whipping and getting caught in her mouth, with that inevitable BIG SMILE people get when boating. Then Dee-dee could replace all those river-boys in my fantasies of getting my breasts fondled on small-town docks. Instead of a dark-faced boy coming up to the boat, putting his hand on my breasts and massaging, it could be Dee-dee.

She waved her hot dog, drawing me from my reverie.

"I have a true story Cat."

The firelight made her face a jack-o-lantern.

"We were living in the city," she began, "and my dad was entrusted with a new find. A baby mummy. He was appointed to remove the wrappings. There was a temperature-controlled room at the university, but Dad took the mummy home to our dining room. Anything could be wrapped in that baby. Rubies, emeralds, scarabs with unknown powers. We had just finished supper. Dad set the mummy on the special unwrapping sheet then stared at the little bundle. He stared for a long time. Robbie was waiting. I was waiting. Mom was waiting. The hands of the clock tick-tocked. Suddenly a crow landed on our windowsill with a great CAW!"

I jumped.

My bossy sister Holly popped out from the behind the tent.

"BOO!"

Dee-dee startled.

Holly bellowed in her deep-booming dad-voice.

"What are you girls doing out here?"

"Yeah, what are you girls doing?" Stringbean's sassy sister Melody popped from the other side with her sour face. "Ha! You girls better watch out. There's a Peeping Tom in the neighborhood. Did you hear about the Peeping Tom, Holly?"

"Yes, Melody," Holly said, "I did hear about that Peeping Tom. I heard he sneaks up on innocent girls and stares at their butts while they're sleeping. Then steals their underwear."

"Oh really?" said Melody. "Well I heard he sneaks up on innocent girls and GIVES THEM A WEDGIE!"

Holly grabbed my swimsuit bottom and tugged up.

Melody went for Dee-dee's bikini.

Dee-dee gave Melody a haunting glare, thrust out her hot dog stick, and hissed, "Stay back! I command you!"

Melody cracked up but backed off, with her syrupy snarl, "Well what have we here? Neighborhood witches? What spells will you be casting tonight, little witches?"

Dee-dee and I kept silent. The time travel was our secret.

Melody gave a nasty sniff.

Holly warned, "You be good!"

Then they were gone.

I pried my bikini from my crack.

"Is it midnight yet?"

Dee-dee checked her windup alarm clock.

"Not yet. Twenty-seven more minutes."

The strained honey marigold and dewdrop mush was baggied in the tent, along with the bacon strips and the wasps. We'd been very careful with those wasps. They'd be difficult to replace. Dee-dee had folded them in a clean paper towel in their own baggie.

As the clock ticked, I stared at the surface of Little Rose. There the moon wavered, a white snake on black water. What if the spell worked? What if we went back to the 1800's? And how would we get back to 1973?

"What if we get stuck there?" I whispered.

"I have done the research," Dee-dee said. "This is what you do to come home."

She bit down on her forefinger.

I bit mine too, for practice.

"Ow."

Dee-dee reached in her knapsack, pulled something ghostly out, and threw it at me.

A pale cloth landed on my face.

"Wear that, Cat. Over your swimsuit. I am wearing one."

She wiggled into a white nightgown with long sleeves and a high lace collar. "So we blend with the era."

I sighed at the nightgown in my hands.

"Go on, Cat. Button up. All the way. Modesty. You do not want to be mistaken for a Lady of the Night."

A Lady of the Night?

Perhaps I did want to be mistaken for a Lady of the Night. Perhaps I wanted some long-ago stranger's dirty hands on my breasts. Perhaps I wanted a young stranger with black eyes and black curls and the blood of slaughtered hogs on his apron to place his dirty hands on my breasts and massage while I fainted in pleasure and fell to the dirt floor of his shop as he hovered over with his hot—

"Button up, Cat!"

Dee-dee shouldered her knapsack.

Something clunked within.

"Gather the ingredients. We need to get going. And fast. Where is the flashlight?"

"What? Going where?"

"To the other side of the lake."

"Why?"

"That is where we need to be. That is where we found the Blacksmith's note. By the ice house."

The old stone foundation.

"But—"

"Come on, Cat! We do not have much time!"

Dee-dee never told me we needed to be on the other side! Oh Dee-dee! I'd been around the woodsy part plenty of times, but never in the dark. And never barefoot—

"Are the batteries working?"

BOOM!

An errant firecracker banged as I flicked on the Eveready. It worked, but no need for the flashlight yet. There was plenty of moonlight out here in the open. We wouldn't need the flashlight till we hit the tangled woods.

"But we're barefoot."

No problem on the grass, but in the woods? With the stickers and berry canes?

"Pain is part of the magic, Cat. So is danger. The potion!"

I leaned in the tent for the baggies.

"Give them to me. Hold the flashlight."

I held the unlit Eveready and Dee-dee pinched the baggies as we crept through Andersons' backyard, past the Northern Pike heads grinning down at us, Mr. Anderson's aluminum boat, the landed ice house, and the spidery woodpile.

At the chain link fence surrounding the next neighbor's yard, I tore my feet on the poking metal. Now I'd have scars on my feet too.

"Ow!"

"Shh!"

After several more backyards we hit the woods. I switched on the light, scared to see what fell in its beam. Rabbit? Snake?

Shriveled face?

Nothing but weeds, trees, and berry-canes.

"Keep moving, Cat! Time is fleeting."

Compelled by the tick-tick of Dee-dee's wind-up clock in her knapsack, I kept moving, though branches tore my hair, brambles tore my hands, and a thorn stuck in my heel.

"Ow!"

"Shh!" warned Dee-dee. "The neighbors must not hear! There must be no witnesses."

No witnesses...

We got through the thickest of the woods and ran down the narrow path along the freeway wall, over the cig butts and empty whiskey bottles of the dangerous Big Snake teens.

I scraped my knees on the storm sewer and tore the shoulder of Dee-dee's nightie by the church.

"Sorry, Dee-dee."

"Do not worry Cat," she whispered as we tiptoed along the lake-edge towards the old stone foundation. "I do not care for that old nightgown. Tear it to shreds when we are done."

Dee-dee fished the clock from her knapsack.

I shone the light on its ticking face.

We sat on the mossy stones listening to the tick-tick. No time to pull the thorn from my screaming heel—

"Almost midnight, Cat! We made it."

We made it. But why couldn't we have stayed on our beach with the Deep Forest OFF and hot dogs and moonlight?

"Ready? We do this in darkness. But first set the potion."

In the flashlight beam Dee-dee opened the baggies and drew out the paper towels with the bacon, honey-mush, and wasps. Carefully she placed the contents atop the wall. As she slowly unfolded the paper towel cradling the wasps, her hand shook, as with the first yellowed note.

"When the alarm goes off, Cat, smear the potion on your tongue, count to one hundred, add the bacon and the wasps and spin thrice. Got that?"

I nodded.

How many times had I spun thrice in my dreams? How many times had I spun for practice with the trees and sky spinning above? How many times had I imagined opening my eyes to the leathery flank of a dinosaur, or the underwater blue of an inland sea, or the great black nothing at the edge of the unformed universe?

Through the tick-tick of the clock, the shush of a car on Big Snake Lake Road, and the low whisper of the freeway, Dee-dee and I stared at each other.

Her blue whirlpools gleamed black, then—

Ring-a-ling-a-ling! Ring-a-ling-a-ling!

Midnight! We moved fast, smearing the honey-paste on our tongues and counting to one hundred.

I had to stay focused, for Dee-dee was counting faster.

"Seventy-nine, seventy-eight, seventy-seven!"

And counting backward! Dee-dee! Would that screw up the charm? No time to ask, I kept counting forward. When I got to one hundred, we picked up the bacon strips, put them under our tongues, and reached for the wasps—

Too dark—

"I canth thee!" I said, my mouth full of bacon.

"I can noth thee ether!" mumbled Dee-dee. "Turnth onth the flathlight, justh for a thekunn."

I felt for the light, aimed at the paper towel, and flashed on Dee-dee's pale face. Strips of flesh hung from her undead lips.

We both grabbed for a stinger, bumped fingers, and put the wasps on our tongues. I clicked off the light.

Should we hold hands? So we stay together?

Too late. Dee-dee was already spinning thrice, the dangling bacon rising from her lips.

"Croak-croak" called a bullfrog. Too late!

I shut my eyes with fear and excitement, and to feel the pull of the spell.

When I opened my eyes, Dee-dee was gone.

NINE

I was alone, surrounded by white. The lake was a flat white expanse. Across the lake, where houses should have been, there rose a snow-covered meadow.

I spun round.

The near shore was a chiaroscuro of black trees and white snow. Snow lay over all. Snow and silence. Silence so loud it hurt. I put my hands over my ears.

Whumph.

What was that?

Snow sliding from a branch?

I was further back in time than the pig farm. There were no barns here, no fences, and no snorting hogs. Nothing but meadow and forest. The spell had worked!

But where was Dee-dee?

"Dee-dee?" I whispered, "Dee-dee Morton?"

I should have been cold, bare-footed in the snow, with just a nightgown over my swimsuit, but I didn't feel the snow under my feet or the frost in my nose or the cold blowing up the nightie. Only the throbbing thorn in my foot.

"Dee-dee?"

"Argh!"

A sound at my feet, where the old ice house should be. There was no ice house. And no stone foundation. Just a big tree. Was I back before the stockyard days? Before the white man?

"Dee-dee?"

The snow beneath the tree began to move.

I gasped in relief. She'd been plopped in a snowbank! I reached out to help her up.

"Dee—"

As the snow fell away I saw it wasn't Dee-dee. It was a mass of matted hair, fur, and wool. An Indian! I'd come back to the time of the Chippewa.

The wriggling thing grunted. Je swee this, sacre blur that! Some guttural French. A nose and cheeks showed under the dangling hat and matted hair. A burp exploded from the lips.

"Ar-guh!"

The eyes stayed shut, the lashes covered in snow, with ice frosting the grizzled cheeks and sideburns.

"Hello?"

No answer, just more grunts.

"Bonjour?"

I knew a little French from Mr. Swanson's class.

"Bon wee? Hello?"

The man seemed not to hear. He burped again, leaned forward, and spewed vomit.

I drew back and held my breath. There was no stink. And no cloud of breath from me. I stomped my feet. No footprints.

So that's how this works, I thought as the Voyageur's vomit steamed. I was back in time, but not like a flesh and blood human. Like a ghost, I left no trace. That was the only way we'd be allowed back. If we didn't upset the Grand Unfolding.

The man in the snow belched again, gave a curse, and dug in the drifts with his bare hands, throwing bottles aside. From under an empty bottle he drew out a small leather pouch. As he held the pouch, cascades of French words poured from his mouth. He brought the pouch to his chest, struggled with the strings, and withdrew one small stone statuette, then another. He held the statuettes in his hands, stroked them, cooed to them.

One statuette was a fat naked woman, her huge breasts

resting atop a protuberant belly, her legs diminishing to tiny points. The other was a naked man with a lion's head. The Frenchman kissed each statuette, put them back in the pouch, pulled the strings and passed out. The pouch fell to the snow.

"Hello?"

He began snoring.

"Bonjour? Mister?"

Snow gathered on his face, hat, and lashes.

"Monsieur?"

I reached for his sleeve, thought better of touching that unwashed mess, and grabbed for the pouch instead.

I got a shock. Ja-ja-zzzzt!

I jerked back. Tried again. Same shock. Ja-ja-zzzzt!

Ah! The rules of time travel. I could look and hear, but could not touch.

And where was Dee-dee? How far did this forest go on? Was it nothing but trees and meadow for miles? Or was there a path leading back to an Indian camp?

Though the snow fell unceasingly, the cold hadn't gotten to me, not at all. I was hot as the August night I'd left behind. The thorn in my heel screamed, my mosquito bites itched. I scratched my forearm, scraping off skin.

The sleeping man moaned.

One last try to rouse him. "Mister? HELLO!"

Something nearby took flight. Something else slithered. What was that, behind the tree?

I bit my forefinger.

The night turned inside out.

The air left my lungs.

I went blind.

The night turned right side out.

My breath came back.

My sight returned.

Dee-dee stood before me panting. On her white nightgown was a dark slash. In her hand was a curved blade. In the moonlight the weapon gleamed with inlaid gems.

There was the old stone foundation. There the houses across the lake. Here the summer night I'd left behind.

"I did it, Cat!" Dee-dee gasped. "Ah!"

"Did what?"

"Killed the Blackguard!"

"You what?"

"I thrust my vorpal sword in! He is a dead man!"

She wiped the sword on the mossy foundation.

"Hah!" Dee-dee heaved. "Hah! He almost got me! And he would have, and could have, but I snuck up! Then I flirted. I bent over and opened my blouse! To here! I showed him some winsome flesh! And I did not give him time to see my trusty weapon. Before he could lay one dirty hand on me, this, I said, is for all the young ladies you buried behind your blacksmith shop. Then I stuck him!"

Dee-dee thrust the sword into the night.

"In his belly, Cat. It felt so good."

She gritted her teeth, "I felt it go in. And you do not know, Cat," she panted, "what it is to live—until you have taken a life."

I swallowed.

"The spell was just right! It sent me back to the perfect time and place. It was a saloon called the Black Bone, and ha!"

I imagined a saloon with a sign hanging painted with one black bone, but I didn't see what was so funny.

Dee-dee bent to catch her breath. Her face shone with sweat. Her nightgown stuck to her breasts.

"Where were you, Cat?"

"I—"

"Why did you not stay by my side?"

"Uh—"

"Oh, you should have seen it!" She peeled the nightgown from her heaving chest. "I am so hot. And thirsty."

I was thirsty too, but not hot. The cold I hadn't felt as I stood in the long-ago snow had caught up with me. I shivered.

"What is the matter, Cat? Your lips are blue."

She reached to touch me.

I stumbled back. "I, I went back to—"

"You went back too? To where?"

Moonlit saliva gleamed at the corners of her mouth.

"To—" I couldn't feel my lips. My teeth began to clink. "Be—before," I stammered, hugging myself.

"Before what, Cat?"

I shrugged.

"Cat, what did you do?"

She lowered her chin.

"Did you disturb the Great Unfolding?"

"No! I did nothing!"

The cold reached my stomach, my mosquito bites screamed, and the thorn in my foot made my eyes water.

"Never mind." Her hand gripped my arm like a firebrand. "Our task is completed."

She slid her sword into her knapsack. Clunk.

I sank to the stone wall and tried to squeeze the thorn from my heel, but couldn't see well enough, and trying made it worse.

We headed back to the tent, with me limping through the brambles and Dee-dee slinging my arm over her shoulder, and if I hadn't been so freezing cold on that July night, and hadn't had the fiery thorn in my heel, and hadn't been shivering from the shock of traveling back hundreds of years, I would've slid my hand along Dee-dee's nightgown and gently cupped her breast.

Instead I sighed and limped.

Afterwards, as I lay in the blue tent with Dee-dee softly breathing beside me, questions buzzed in my brain. Where had that fancy sword come from? How had Dee-dee gone back to exactly the right time and place? And how did she get the power to stab the Evil Blacksmith, when I couldn't even grab hold of a little leather pouch?

Next morning, over Pop Tarts, I asked.

"Dee-dee," I said as margarine melted into my pastry-holes, "how did you stick the knife in?"

"Like this." She parried her fork with a squishing sound. "Squoink. The blade went right in."

"But how did you—"

"How did I what, Cat?"

Never mind, I shrugged.

I was exhausted.

The cold from the snow had burrowed deep in my bones, the thorn in my foot screamed through a nerve to my jaw, and Dee-dee had a deadly sparkle in her eyes like the gems in that curved blade.

"Also," she said, "I pressed Tess into the arms of Mush Boy."

"What?"

She wiped a gleam of margarine from her cheek.

"I wanted to tell you last night, Cat, but you were in such a perilous state I waited till morning. I saw them in the town as I was leaving the Black Bone. He was out by the horses with a slop of mush—"

"A slop? Of mush?"

"A slop of mush, Cat. A mush bucket! A bucket of mush! The Mush Boy was out there with a bucket of mush, and she was there too, shyly standing around, lifting her skirt daintily over a puddle. It was Tess! And he was about to kneel before her to cover the puddle with his cape, and I thought, this is a perfect moment to press Tess into the arms of the Mush Boy!"

I swallowed.

"I did it, Cat! I lit under my chin with the flashlight like a ghoul and said, I am a ghost from the future and I do MARRY ye with all the blessings of the twentieth century! Then I pressed Tess into the arms of the Mush Boy. They kissed right there in the street, then we went back in the tavern to toast their wedded bliss. I got them both a flagon of grog and we drank to their conjugal happiness. The Evil Blackguard was stone dead by then right where I had left him, in a pool of blood on the tavern floor, and all the townsfolk were celebrating his demise and heralding the marriage and the barkeep was giving free grog to all. We did it!"

Dee-dee bit into her Cinnamon Pop Tart.

"Mission accomplished."

I shifted in my seat.

Very funny. You are so funny, Dee-dee.

"What?" She gave me her big-eyed grin. "What, Cat?"

The thorn came out next week. A pocket of pus developed and out it popped, just like Mom said it would. Give it time, she said, and Mom was right. I stepped from the tub, wiped my foot, and there it was on the towel, a tiny black claw.

I saved that claw-like thorn in my jewelry box to remind me of our time-travel night. Maybe Dee-dee had gone back in time, but why were the rules of time travel so different for her? And when would we time travel again?

I wasn't keen on it. The cold from that night had settled in my bones like a long, slow song of long-dead folks.

What happened to my drunken Voyageur? Did he freeze on the shore? Or trudge back to an Indian camp with his pouch of statuettes? And what about Dee-dee? Soon she would turn sixteen. Would she then leave me for the dangerous Big Snake Lake teens?

After killing the Evil Blacksmith, Dee-dee became jubilant. Her anger vanished. In its place came unstoppable wildness. We had a sleepover for her birthday, just she and I huddled in the dark corner of her basement, lit by candlelight, with crème de menthe, a jumbo bag of Cheetos, and the Ouija board. The gliding planchette wrote across the Ouija, *STOP MEDDLING IN WHAT YOU DO NOT UNDERSTAND.*

I'd gotten chills from those words, but Dee-dee just laughed. "Oh those spirits!" she laughed, "What do they know! Who understands anything? It is all mystery! Stop meddling in what you do not understand? Very funny, spirits!"

She put her face close to mine, and with each hot puff of breath, scented with Cheetos and crème de menthe, she said, "If no one meddled in what they did not understand we would not have pyramids! Or printing presses! Or light bulbs! Or moon-landings! Or poetry! Or pancakes!"

She went on with her endless list and with each thing named, Dee-dee threw a handful of Cheetos into the dark basement.

But all I heard were the words of the Ouija.

Stop meddling in what you do not understand.

What I didn't understand were those Poison Pens that kept blooming in our mailboxes. Tammy had gotten three more (which we intercepted).

Dear Whore, you are still in that bikini!
Dear Whore, I see your blaspheming bosoms!
Dear Whore, SINNERS BURN IN HELL

Then Dee-dee got a Poison Pen:

Dear Hippie, comb your hair! Invest in a barrette!
This is not a flower child commune!

Dee-dee just sneered, shook her locks, buried her hairbrush down by the lake, and let her hair go wild the rest of the summer. I ran wild with her. We danced around bonfires, chanted spells to curse the Poison Pen, and concocted magical tinctures to make bossy Holly and sassy Melody suffer grievously.

And Dee-dee taught me to shoplift.

Well she tried.

One hot August afternoon she lolled on her bed with a tray of ice cubes and wriggled her fingers.

"See these hands, Cat? These are the hands of a shoplifter."

"What?"

"You are the distractor. I am the lifter of goods."

She gathered her hair into a golden bundle, popped an ice cube from the tray and ran it along her neck.

"Shoplifting, Cat. I have a long history. You will be training with the very best. My Auntie Cindy was a shoplifter. She trained me downtown. At Dayton's."

She slid the ice slowly over her collarbone.

The cold raised her nipples.

I swallowed spit.

"Dayton's is where it began, Cat. I had my heart set on a white sweater with red strawberries, and Auntie Cindy would not get it for me. But I really wanted that sweater. So I threw a tantrum. And while I tantrumed, Auntie stole the sweater."

I turned and stared at our drawings on the wall, of Tess, Mush Boy, and Dee-dee on fire.

"Thereafter," Dee-dee said, "every time we went to Dayton's

I had a tantrum, and Auntie shoplifted. That was a boom year."

The bedsprings keened as she got up.

I didn't turn to watch Dee-dee sit cross-legged over her cigar box to roll a joint.

As she inhaled the freshly-lit joint, her mom opened the front door, home early.

"Dee-dee? Robbie?"

Dee-dee coughed out, "At Zipper's."

"What?"

"ROBBIE IS AT ZIPPER'S!"

"Okay! I'm going to Red Owl."

"Okay!"

Sound of the front door shutting.

Dee-dee blew out smoke.

"My mother is not going to Red Owl."

"What?"

I turned and sat up.

"My mother is having an affair," Dee-dee picked at her lip. "With a math professor. They met at some conference."

I shrugged to hide my horror.

"I listen," Dee-dee nodded, "on the phone. My dad too. With one of his students. It is old news."

I felt sick, imagining how I'd feel if one of my parents were having an affair. Mom would never. Dad would never. The broken home, fallen on its side, with darkness seeping out.

"Back to the subject at hand." Dee-dee shaved ash into a peanut butter jar lid. "Shoplifting. After that first tantrum, Auntie Cindy trained me. We had a code word. Pumpernickel. Auntie went to the makeup counter. The makeup lady helped her. I stood by Auntie's side. Auntie said, oh this smells like carnations. This smells like violets. This looks like gingerbread. Or doe-skin. Or pumpernickel. When I heard the code word, I threw myself down and tantrumed."

I imagined Dee-dee in petticoats face-down on the red carpet of Dayton's, her tiny hands in fists, tiny feet kicking.

"I had a system. I would hold my breath until I could hold it no longer, then let loose with a scream to blast the whole department. All eyes on me, crying my heart out."

She held out the joint.

I shook my head as usual.

"We did it again and again. Oh, this reminds me of lemons, Auntie would say, this is like cucumber, this is pumpernickel."

Dee-dee let out a puff of smoke.

"You and I shall use the same code word, Cat."

I turned back to the wall.

Under a drawing of Tess, my pencil sketch of Dee-dee burning at the stake quivered.

"But you will not be throwing a tantrum, Cat. Maybe you can have an epileptic fit. Or perhaps faint. But I think best would be if you got sick to your stomach."

The pencil drawing of Dee-dee at the stake came alive, the flames flickering in a tiny pencil way.

"But you will not be getting sick, Cat. You will bring a can of Campbell's Cream of Mushroom Soup and a can opener. You will open the soup in the Ladies' Room, and you will put a big mouthful in and hold it while I shop. Can you do that? I think you can."

The gray Persian leapt on the bed, touched its nose to my leg, and settled against my feet, purring.

"You can practice holding a mouthful," Dee-dee followed the cat, climbed on the bed and pressed against me, her breasts to my back. "I can help you."

I froze, terrified of getting what I wanted—

And terrified of ruining the moment.

"You do comprehend," Dee-dee whispered in my ear, "I will be at the makeup counter, and have all the makeup out, the eyeshadow, lipstick, and blush, and you will be behind me with the mushroom soup in your mouth, and I will say pumpernickel, and you will throw up, so to speak."

"You don't even like makeup, Dee-dee."

"No, I do not."

"Then why steal it?"

She said she would be stealing for me, as I had a desire for cosmetics, and my pencil sketch of Dee-dee quietly screamed in the soundless scream of the damned.

We did try.

The next day we took the bus to Dayton's and I went to the Ladies' Room and poured a can of mushroom soup into my mouth and held it there and suffered greatly as Dee-dee took her time at the makeup counter till she had the raspberriest red, shimmeriest blue, and ripest green. When my mouth could hold the soup no longer and my jaw ached and eyes watered, Dee-dee said, "Oh look at this eyeshadow, such a fine shade of taupe, do you think this makes me look like the wing of a dove? Or a blossoming lily? Or a slice of pumpernickel?"

Then BLAT! I let the soup go on Dayton's red carpet.

But I couldn't bear the thought of stealing.

THOU SHALT NOT.

Before she could palm up one eyeshadow I grabbed Dee-dee's arm and dragged her from the store.

I was a failure as a shoplifter.

I could not do it.

I was also a failure at kissing Dee-dee.

As she reached for the Coppertone while sun-tanning down at the lake, I tried to press my lips to hers, but instead fell face-first onto her greased belly. When she was putting on her swimsuit in our bathroom, I saw her two womanly wonders in the mirror and my mouth dove to her breast, but just then she raised her elbow and gave me a bloody lip. During a late-night *Dracula* as Bela Lugosi was about to bite into a pale neck, I snuck my lips towards Dee-dee's throbbing throat, but she coughed in screaming laughter and spit out a Cheeto.

At every opportunity I was too fast or too slow, or too near or too far to kiss Dee-dee. And whenever I imagined our lips meeting and all the bright burning that would surely ensue, I'd remember the long-ago Brunette Breck Girl trapped behind our basement bathroom tiles. THOU SHALT NOT. Shoplifting was bad, but shoplifting was nothing compared to girl-kissing.

Girl-kissing made you a Lezbo. And Lezbo meant Freak. And freaks were cast out of White Rock. *Cast out or worse.*

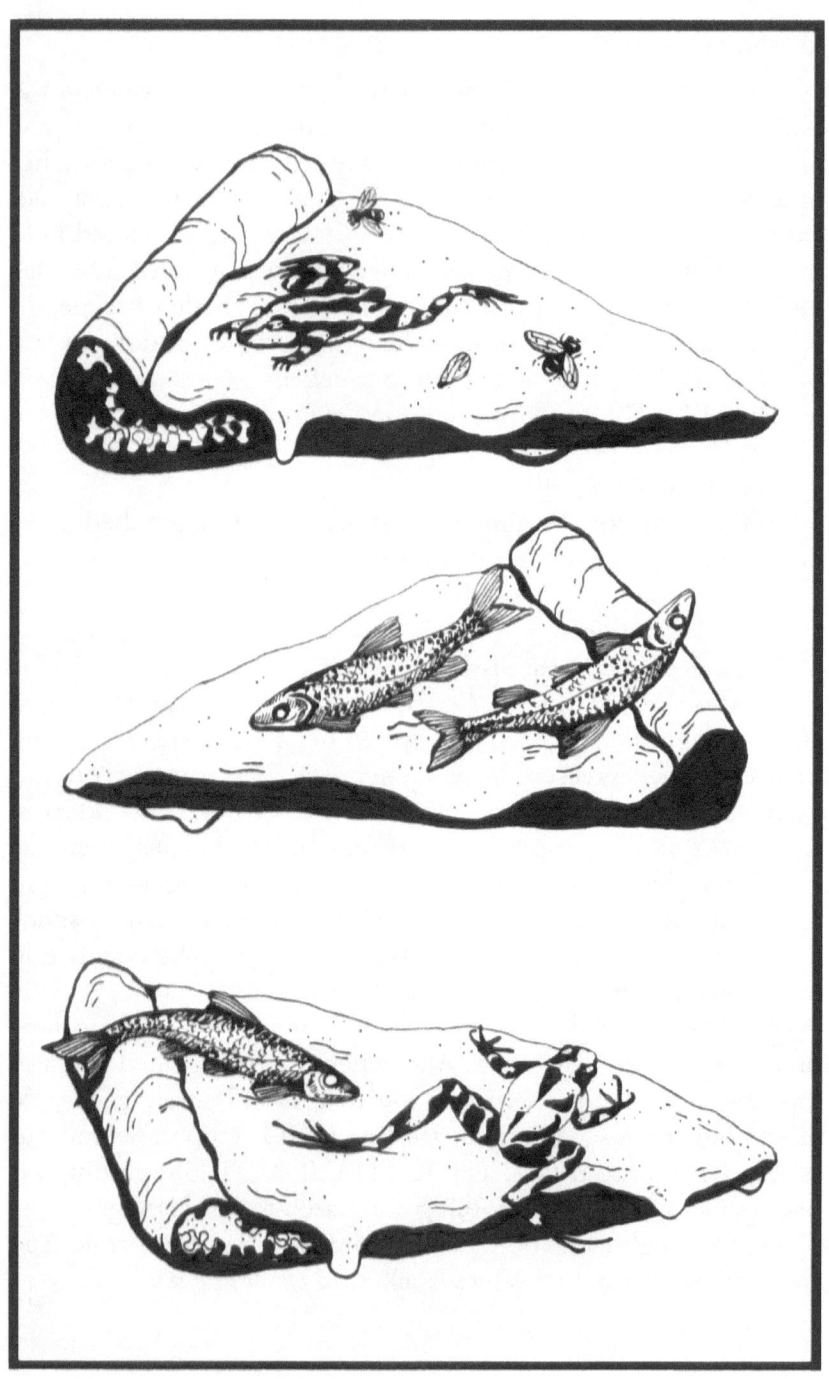

TEN

August 23, 1973 was our last summer sleepover.

Bossy Holly and sassy Melody were having a boy-girl party at our house. Mom and Dad were boating on the river. It was the time of the mayfly, when millions of the fairy-like insects mated mid-air over the Mississippi then died, covering the water with their tiny brown corpses.

But there were no mayflies around us—

And no parents—

Dee-dee's dad was long gone, her mom was at some divorced women's getaway, and crybaby Robbie was crying again. Robbie was supposed to have a sleepover with Zipper Zupinski, but for some reason Zipper couldn't come. All the better for us. Let Robbie mope alone down in the basement. Dee-dee and I were ready for fun.

We made cheeseburgers on the grill, had a six pack of Dr. Pepper, and Dee-dee snuck a twenty from her mom's purse and ordered two large pepperonis with extra cheese.

Robbie wasn't hungry. He picked up one slice, set it back on his plate, and stared out the window. There was nothing out that window. No swing set, no garden, no clothesline. Just empty backyard. Robbie Morton was staring at nothing.

I used to stare at nothing. I used to go fuzzy in Mom's lap, listening to her voice reverberate as my fingers traced the tiny scars on her hands, those little shut mouths I knew had secrets sealed inside. And at suppertime I'd disappear without knowing, till Dad brought me back with his pounding and shouting— WHAT THE HELL'S WRONG WITH CAT?

Then I'd run down to the lake and stare at the water with my wishes: *Let me turn into a real-live mermaid. Let the bratty twins dry up and die. Let the waters of Little Rose be sucked up in a whirlwind so the bottom is laid bare. Let the bottom be laid bare!*

And let me have another slice of pizza.

I could have used one of Robbie's. I was watching his slices closely. My intent was to be fair, but when it comes to eating, I could finish a whole double-cheese easy, all by myself.

Robbie was staring and Dee-dee was chewing when I got this sick feeling. It wasn't the pizza. It was something else. I kept thinking about that first yellowed note Dee-dee had pulled from the crack in our front steps.

Something was wrong there. Something obvious. Sometimes the obvious isn't obvious to me. I kept eating. The sick feeling was below my stomach. Maybe the sick feeling was Dee-dee. Dee-dee was on fire that night. I wondered if she'd popped a pill from the medicine cabinet or from her mom's purse. She hadn't brought out the pot yet, not in front of Robbie, but she was high on something. I could tell by that shiny look in her eyes, a fish out of water.

She raised her eyebrows to get my attention. From under the table she joggled a small bottle of brown liqueur. Perhaps she'd put that in her pop. And in mine? And in Robbie's?

Robbie was still staring into space. His tears had dried up. His face was white stone. He took one bite of pizza and forgot to chew. With the lump in his cheek he left the table.

"More, Robbie?" I asked his back.

He walked away without speaking.

"Guess that means no!" Dee-dee burst out laughing.

A bit of pepperoni flew from her mouth, hitting the last sample box of Cap'n Crunch.

I laughed too, but wasn't really laughing. I washed Robbie's slices down with a sip of pop, but something was wrong that night. Something invisible. Perhaps the mummy's curse was finally coming home. Perhaps my vacant lot curse was coming home. Perhaps it was the sound of the dehumidifier running day and night for the mummy.

Whatever it was it passed. I burped and farted, and what I felt below my stomach gave way and went deeper, down to the mystery cave where Dee-dee and I explored the underworld in a chalk canoe.

For the rest of that night, instead of hanging out with the Ouija board in the basement, Dee-dee and I sat on the floor of her darkened bedroom, lit candles, and listened to *Tony Scott's Music for Zen Meditation.*

Hare Krishna, Hare-Hare...

As I drifted with the music, Dee-dee found *The Egyptian Book of the Dead.*

"Cat," she said, "I think you should borrow this."

I shrugged.

"Just in case," she pulled a strand of hair from her mouth, "death comes to find you."

The book was soft with use. Inside the yellow cover were poetic hieroglyphics above their translations. *Golden limbs, my mother twice, my heart of coming into being,* along with endless chants for dead bodies not to be torn up, cast in the sea, or eaten by dogs.

Let not my penis be assundered from me.

Very funny, Dee-dee.

I slid *The Book of the Dead* into my sleeping bag, and as the candles burned down, between sips of liqueur, we read ancient poems by the Greek poetess Sappho. Only bits and pieces remained, Dee-dee said, on torn papyrus and broken pottery. We took turns.

Leaving your father's golden home...
In my wild heart I most wish...
Let me back into the harness of your love...

As I read, Dee-dee drew a small pipe from her cigar box.

"You are in for a real treat tonight, Cat."

She unpacked a small wad of Reynold's Wrap.

From the aluminum foil she drew out a velvety-green chunk. She placed the chunk in her pipe, flicked her Bic, inhaled and passed it to me.

The liqueur had made me both light and heavy. I already felt in a dream. What the heck, I thought, light me up, Dee-dee.

It was finally time to inhale.

I drew on the pipe. The smoke burned like velvet on fire, coating my lungs with luxuriant pain. I coughed and coughed and could not stop. The coughing made me dizzy.

I leaned against the side of Dee-dee's bed.

What the hell, I thought. Hit me again.

Then said it aloud, "Hit me again, Dee-dee."

Hit me where my wild heart most wishes.

In the time it took to lean back, my voice had grown deeper. My legs throbbed. A tight fire had been lit in my thighs. Another fire burned somewhere. In Dee-dee's eyes.

As our drawings of Tess and Mush Boy danced in the candlelight by my pencil sketch of Dee-dee burning at the stake, I climbed fist over fist onto her bed, and in the hollow once occupied by the mummy, curled in a fetal position and fell asleep.

When I woke Dee-dee was all over me.

Her hands were on my waist and on my budding breasts and in the fork of my legs. Her breath was in my eyes and in my ears and in my nose. She was fighting me. She was wrestling.

Then her open mouth was on mine.

I froze. Dee-dee froze. With her open mouth on mine we both froze. The only thing moving was our breath, back and forth into each other.

Dee-dee pulled away and leaned on her elbow.

The few candles that hadn't drowned in their own wax flickered thickly.

Dee-dee's eyes were black hollows, her hair lava.

She licked her lips.

"Hi Cat. How are you doing?"

I shrugged.

"I am fine, Dee-dee. How are you?"

She raised her hand as if to hypnotize.

"I am crazy-mad about you, Cat."

Her fingers swam to me, rivered down my t-shirt, and barely touched my nipple. She squeezed oh-so-slowly, all the while looking in my eyes. Something glimmered in hers. Something I wanted, and a red-hot wire ran from my nipple to my hips.

Then we made out. Really made out. Like in the movies only better. Better because we were both girls. Better because our legs entangled perfectly. We got locked together and could not get free. I was suffocating. Dee-dee was killing me. She was killing me with her lips and her breath and her breasts. And I was killing Dee-dee. I was killing Dee-dee with my hips and my shoulders and my thighs. The whole weight of me rocked against her. I was holding her down, I was drowning her. We were killing each other. Our mouths were locked in silent screams, and the candles were drowning in molten wax, and the air was going in and coming out, going in and coming out, and nothing was going to save us.

Part Two

Waking Up

ELEVEN

Instead of waking in Dee-dee's bed, I woke in the middle of Little Rose Lake. Alone I sat in a white chalk canoe. The canoe glowed with the light of an oncoming storm. The sky was swollen purple, the lake was mirror-glass, the birds silent. Nothing stirred on the far shore. No lawnmowers hummed, no kids ran down, no blue jay screamed *danger-danger!*

Dee-dee's head broke the water—just the very top—her sopping blond locks brown as chocolate. That anonymous circle reminded me of a baby about to be born, the damp skull just crowning the mother, the hairs curled from maternal fluids, that moment when you don't know what's coming next. Will it be a boy or a girl? Will it be perfect, or will it be a freak?

Careful not to tip the canoe, I bent towards Dee-dee, but instead of helping her up, I placed my hand atop her head and pushed down. Solid as stone, her head went under. She didn't fight. Not much. Not like I fought when the bratty twins who couldn't swim used me as a ladder, so I knew how Dee-dee felt as the white circle of water closed over, her last look at sky, the silent scream, the gush and suck from light to dark, the green all round and the silence after.

But if I kill her now, I thought, I'll wake from this dream and never see what happens next.

I relaxed my grip.

Dee-dee's face came up shining. I grasped her wrist. She rose bare-breasted. Up came the rest of her, her bottom half clothed in scales. Her cumbrous tail came up—splat. Her tailfin, wide as Mr. Anderson's rake, filled the space between us. All of mermaid Dee-dee sat in the chalk canoe.

She squirmed to situate, rested her elbows on the gunwales, and spoke in that throaty whisper.

"You may ask me now, Cat."

"Ask you what?"

"What you have been yearning to ask me all summer."

I glanced up at the gathering storm. What had I been yearning to ask all summer? Why is your brother Robbie always crying? Are your mom and dad really both having affairs? Can I stay in your bed curled up with you forever?

What was I yearning to ask?

When you stop wondering about something, when you push it down deep, so even you can't reach, then it's hard to talk about when you finally get a chance to speak.

I shrugged.

"Repeat after me," she said, "where."

"Where," I echoed.

"Where did."

"Where did."

"You get."

"You get—"

That brown and desiccated thing.

I coughed on the fountaining words.

"Where did you get that mummy, Dee-dee?"

"Shush."

She put a finger to her lips.

Silent lightning flashed beyond the freeway wall.

A big storm over Big Snake.

"This must be," Dee-dee said, "our secret."

TWELVE

There I was, in the middle of Little Rose Lake with mermaid Dee-dee in the chalk canoe, her skin palest jade, her hair clinging to her breasts, her knuckles white, gripping the gunwales.

She drew a breath.

Blood-red gills opened along her neck.

Can she breathe air, I wondered. How long can she stay alive out of the water? And how far will this dream-canoe take me before I wake?

Dee-dee flared her nostrils and began.

"Long before I met you, Cat, the mummy came. I was with Dad in the city. We were looking for a new place to live by the university. We stood on the steps of an old rose-colored stone apartment. The caretaker came out to greet us. He and Dad talked in the sunlight. They talked on and on. I waited for them to stop talking, so we could go in and see the place, but they kept talking, so I went in by myself, through two pairs of heavy doors, up a wide staircase to the first landing where dust motes danced in the sun. I paused for a moment to watch the dust rise and fall, then went up to the third floor alone. No one was out in the hallways. No sound came from behind the closed doors. I stopped at number 317, the apartment we had come to see, put my hand on the knob and entered, expecting to find the place empty, filled with sunlight and my echoing footsteps. Instead the place was dim and heavily draped and my footsteps were hindered by boxes—dusty boxes of every size and shape stacked everywhere, haphazardly. I squeezed through the boxes to the dining room. Atop the table was a narrow box draped in dark cloth. As I brushed past, the cloth slipped to the floor, rousing a cloud of dust, and revealing a glass case. I wet my finger to wipe a circle in the glass. A voice boomed, LIFT THE LID! There was no one else in the apartment. LIFT THE LID! the voice bellowed. Such a commanding voice! I must obey. I lifted the lid. Inside was the very thing you saw on my bed, remember, Cat? The rigid limbs? The empty eyeholes? Your first look at the mummy. You fainted. I woke you with a kiss. But my first sight of that mummy! No sooner had I raised the glass than the disembodied voice said, GET THE TISSUE! I looked around. Nearby sat a box of tissue. No sooner had I drawn a tissue than the voice said, PUT IT IN WATER! There sat a glass of water. I dipped the tissue. PUT IT ON MY EYE! I rushed the dripping tissue to the mummy and placed it on the empty eye. Immediately the eye opened—alive, cobalt, bluest blue. MY OTHER! I drew out another tissue, dipped, and placed it on the other eye. It bloomed alive. MY SKIN! boomed the voice. I pulled out more tissue, dipped, and placed it on the mummy. Under each dripping tissue the skin came alive. MORE! I drew, dipped, and placed. Finally there on the table breathed not a mummy, but a blue-eyed boy. Just then I heard voices in the hall. Dad and the caretaker! I wrapped the boy in the cloth, walked him to a back bedroom, and hid with him behind boxes, holding my breath till the caretaker left. What could I do? Keep the boy hidden? Leave him behind? As an Egyptologist, Dad had heard stranger tales of mummies coming back to life. I showed Dad the boy and told him the tale. But what could we do? Send the boy to a museum? Give him to the caretaker? We took him home and concocted a story. He was my little brother. With a speech impediment. We taught him how to speak a few words, and sent him to school. As a problem learner. And there *was* a problem. He had powers. At dinner he would float up to the ceiling. And he could move things. Just by looking at them. Like Uri Geller. That was fine at home, but not at school. Do not use your powers at school, we said. No flying off. No floating up. Stay at your desk. For a while he was normal. But not at night. At night he'd pace in a robe of scarlet and purple, embroidered with all the planets—all night in the living room he'd pace chanting in ancient Egyptian. Then one day walking home from school, he and I came upon two boys, one stuck in a tree, the other below crying for help. He floated right up, got the boy down, and set him on the ground. Both boys' mouths dropped open and they ran off. I knew then he must not go on. He could not do such things. Not out in the open. No saving kids. No flying up. And no more school. They will take you away, we said, lock you up, do experiments on you. So we locked him in. He slept all day and paced all night, chanting in that robe. Each day he grew thinner. Then he stopped pacing. Then stopped eating. Then took to his bed. He would not move. Would not take one bite of food, nor one sip of water. Then one morning I woke with an empty feeling, and looked under the sheets—and he was gone. There was just the crust of him, all dried up, back the way he used to be.

"And that," said mermaid Dee-dee through her lips blue with breathlessness, "is where the mummy came from."

CRACK!

The sky cracked with lightning.
One loud crack—
The canoe shuddered.

Dee-dee slipped over the gunwale and was gone. Instantly Little Rose came alive with splatters. The rain poured so thickly I couldn't see where Dee-dee had slipped in. Rain stabbed my eyes. Rain stung my cheeks. Rain began to fill the chalk canoe. I had nothing to bail with but my hands. I bailed and bailed with cupped hands but rainwater filled as quickly as I bailed, and rain began to dissolve the chalk canoe. My eyes watered, my nose ran, and my fingers went numb as I tried to save the dissolving canoe, tried to smooth it back to the way it used to be, but no use. I bailed and bailed and smoothed and smoothed but the rain filled and the walls dissolved and what was left of my perfect chalk canoe sank into the waters of Little Rose.

THIRTEEN

I sobbed out loud.

My sob woke me.

I was naked in Dee-dee's bed, tangled in the sea of sheets we'd tussled in the night before, our last summer sleepover. Still feeling the chalk of my dream canoe dissolving under my hands, I untangled from the sheets and sat up.

"Dee-dee?"

I heard the dehumidifier running for the mummy in her dad's study, but no Dee-dee.

I pulled on my underwear and t-shirt, blinked to the bathroom, then into the hall.

"Dee-dee?"

I whispered, so as not to wake her mom, then remembered Mrs. Morton was away at some Divorced Women's Getaway. She was probably crying in a circle with other divorced moms, using up boxes and boxes of kleenex.

I swallowed as I descended the six steps to the kitchen.

My mouth tasted of dead pizza and lakewater.

What a night we'd had, Dee-dee and I!

Dare I speak of it?

Dare I recount the tastes and smells we'd encountered in each other's nakedness?

Dee-dee sat at the kitchen table by the last sample box of

Cap'n Crunch, staring straight ahead, as Robbie had stared the night before. Three crusts of leftover pizza sat on the grease-spotted cardboard by Robbie's flat pop.

"Morning," I said, picking out a grain of sleep.

She didn't answer.

"Dee-dee?"

The kitchen faucet let forth one drip.

Was she going to talk to me? We'd done something wonderful and terrible in her bed last night. THOU SHALT NOT. Would we now be put into blenders, two huge Osterizers side by side, Dee-dee and I naked in each, our noses to the glass, mouthing *this is goodbye, kid?*

"Dee-dee?"

I touched her arm. It was stone cold.

"Dee-dee? Are you going to talk to me?"

I sat down and stared at the last orange and blue sample cereal box with the smiling sea captain till the colors blurred. The vinyl of the kitchen chair stuck to my thighs.

"Dee-dee? I just had the most, it was the weirdest—"

How could I tell her about that dream, she a mermaid, the boy-mummy, and my poor dissolving chalk canoe?

"Dee-dee? Are you mad at me?"

"In the basement," she said, her eyes dull, her voice flat.

"What?"

"The basement."

She bit her lip, so hard I feared she'd puncture it.

"What about the basement, Dee-dee?"

No answer.

"Dee-dee, what about it?"

A tiny red river ran down her chin.

I unstuck my thighs and stumbled towards the basement.

At the head of the stairs I felt for the light switch.

I wasn't scared of Dee-dee's basement. Dee-dee's basement wasn't like our basement. Dee-dee's basement didn't flood, have spiders and centipedes, or smell of mold and mildew.

Our basement was musty and damp. Our basement flooded during summer thunderstorms. Our basement smelled of mildew, and some of the bathroom tiles, with their swirls of brunette hair, had fallen off so you could see through to the raked yellow-brown glue. And our basement had a human skull atop my big sisters' dresser.

It's not a real skull, my sisters said back when I was a wee one. It's a replica. *Rep-lick-uh*. It was the first time I'd heard the word, so they'd explained carefully. A replica meant a copy, a fake, something not real made to look like something real. That skull was a gift from a big sister's Science Museum boyfriend. Once part of an exhibit, it was cast in Plaster of Paris from a real human skull and painted dingy yellow-ochre, as if buried for ages. My sisters might call it a replica but it was real to me. A real cast from a real human skull was real to me. I knew if I went down to our basement alone, and went into my big sisters' bedroom alone, and climbed on their bed I would see, atop their dresser, beside the lighters, lipstick, and wadded kleenex, that skull with its gaping eyeholes. And I knew if I looked into those eyeholes that skull would lock me in its gaze. And when it locked me in its gaze it would talk to me in a voice from the grave. And when it talked to me in its voice from the grave it would tell me things little girls weren't supposed to know. So I never went into my big sisters' bedroom alone and never climbed on their bed alone and never looked in that skull's eyes ever.

But one bright morning I woke to an empty house. I sat up in bed, rubbed my eyes, checked to see if I'd wet the bed, then went to the kitchen. No Mom at the sink. No Holly. No Tammy. Mom? Holly? Tammy? I looked out the back window, called out the front door, shouted downstairs. Were they waiting around the corner to jump out and say BOO? I headed downstairs. No one by the hanging clothes. No one by the tool bench. No one in the laundry room. Not behind the furnace, under the musty couch, or in the fireplace. And no one in the bathroom but the Brunette Breck Girl breathing silently. I entered the big sisters' bedroom. There was the dresser. There the bed. I climbed up. I pushed at the sheets. No one there. On the high dresser sat the skull. Staring at me. Silently. Silent for now. *Silent for now.* But in a moment, when my scent reached its hidey-hole in the deep below, when it sniffed with its long-buried nostrils the scent of a little girl left all alone, then its spirit would rush up quicksilver through the earth, through the roots and mud, the pig-farm blood, burnt bones and beetles, and flood into the skull.

I felt the long-dead whisper coming. The light shifted. There it was in the morning sun, inhabiting the skull, exhaling the grave. LITTLE GIRL! The voice of cracked bird skulls, disintegrating floorboards, and dead centipedes. LITTLE GIRL! You woke me! I flew up! You are not alone! You are with all the souls! Of all the dead! Of all the ages! We are all down here! The slaves and Injuns and babies, the dead of strangling and jealousy, of old age and broken hearts, the mangled and thrashed, the beheaded and drowned. We are all down here waiting for you. We hear your heart beat and feel your breath move, and we shall share with you the secrets of the horrors under—the skin-splitting, tongue-rotting, aching-yearning of the long dead! And the vengeance brewing in us—oh, vengeance, little girl! The dry burning in the cellars of our hearts! And regret! Regret fills our empty heads in the halls of the Underworld! Do not look away! This is Death speaking! Meet my gaze. For if you look away and turn your back and run upstairs I will COME SNAPPING AFTER! Tears exploded from my eyes. Mount Vesuvius erupted from my nose. A scream broke my throat. Through choking sobs I screamed into the skull's eyeholes without cease as the skull hissed on about rage, vengeance, and regret. That's where Tammy found me, centuries later (or half an hour) choking on sobs and staring into the eyes of that replica atop my big sisters' dresser in our mildewy basement.

Dee-dee's basement was nothing like that.

I flicked on the switch at the head of Dee-dee's stairs and went down. Clean, bright, and modern, that was Dee-dee's basement. Shiny black linoleum floor tiles flecked with bits of red and yellow, a built-in bar with a lit-up sign of a glimmering lake, *LAND OF SKY BLUE WATERS*, a couch with throw pillows, a coffee table with magazines, a shelf of board games, Monopoly, Clue, Scrabble. A foosball and pool table.

Stylish, clean, and quiet, that was Dee-dee's basement, and smaller than ours, so the light at the top of the stairs lit the whole space but for one dark corner. No skulls, spiders, or corpses down here.

On the rare occasion we played a lackluster game of foosball, a few tosses into the middle and then done, Dee-dee's basement was noisy, but it was usually quiet, the pool table whispery-soft, the balls rolling over the green felt dropping soundlessly into the holes, and with the magazines, you could turn on the standing lamp, put your feet up, and read in that nice cool quiet.

In the one dark corner where the light didn't reach (where we did the Ouija Board) there was usually nothing but the usual chill of a basement. But today instead of the Ouija Board in that far corner, there was a faceless corpse sitting on the floor wrapped in Dee-dee's orange hippie shawl.

No! Ha-ha! Not a faceless corpse!

Just a joke of Zipper and Robbie's. They'd stuffed boy-clothes and wrapped them in Dee-dee's shawl. Very funny ha-ha! *Very funny Dee-dee.* She sent me down here to scare me.

Well I wasn't scared. I got a taste in my mouth like the faint copper tang of a penny, but I wasn't scared. I'd stared death in the face long ago with that human skull. What did I fear in some faceless dummy? Try harder, Dee-dee. Try harder to scare me. Make me faint again and wake me with a kiss.

Perhaps she'd have a nice surprise waiting for me upstairs. Perhaps that was why she sent me down. Perhaps she'd kiss me when I came back up, like she kissed me last night, that long, grinding kiss that lasted till we both fell asleep.

Or perhaps she was making breakfast up there. Perhaps pancakes and sausages were waiting for me. I was getting tired of Cap'n Crunch. Perhaps Dee-dee was wearing an apron and holding a spatula with her hair pinned back and sizzling pans snapping on the stove. Perhaps she was cracking eggs, stirring batter, picking up slippery fingers of meat and dropping them in, sizzle-sizzle, and soon I'd hear the popping sausage and smell the tangy smoke. Then I'd head back up.

But right now I wasn't going to give her the satisfaction. She hadn't scared me. Not one bit. And I was still sleepy, and just in undies and t-shirt, with my teeth unbrushed and hair uncombed.

I flicked on the standing lamp, sat on the couch and blinked at the magazines. At home we had magazines, but not *Ms.* The cover had a smiling woman with big white teeth. *THE BEAUTY QUEEN WHO WOULDN'T.*

What wouldn't that beauty queen do?

Pose naked for Playboy? French kiss a boy? *Kiss a girl?*

I paged through, then glanced at that silly dummy in the dark corner.

Very funny Dee-dee.

Maybe they'd planned it together, Dee-dee, Robbie, and Zipper. Maybe they were all in on the joke. Maybe that's why Zipper flaked out last night. Maybe while Robbie was acting sad over pizza, Zipper was down here constructing the dummy and Dee-dee lent them her hippie shawl and now they were all in the kitchen cracking up and waiting for me to scream.

I wasn't smelling any delicious breakfast. I was tasting something on my tongue. Something coppery. Metallic. I was tasting pennies. Very funny Dee-dee, placing that faceless dummy and wrapping your shawl around it.

I didn't have any idea how to act with her now that we'd kissed each other all over. What were we going to do next? Get engaged? Run away? Get burned at the stake? Pretend it never happened?

I glanced again at that dummy in the pool of shadow. My curiosity got the better of me, and it was tasting more and more like sucking on a penny down there in Morton's basement, but there was no penny in my mouth.

I turned towards the dummy. In the semi-circle of darkness around the dummy were a dozen sheets of crumpled paper. I walked to the dark corner, lifted one of the papers, took it to the couch, smoothed it out, and held it under the standing lamp.

The page in my hand was translucent onionskin.

In the light I saw the typeface was familiar.

I'd studied it before in the slanting light of the haunted truck and under Mr. Morton's magnifying glass. That typeface was identical to the poison pen letters to Tammy. It had the same missing tail on the lower case g.

The letter read:

Robbie Morton,

You are a FAGGOT!
I know of your HOMOSEXUAL ways. I know of
your blaspheming SIN. I have seen your leering
FACE. I have heard your SICK attempts to lure my
boys into BLASPHEMY. I see the FAGGOTY way
you move your wrists. I see your crybaby face. I
would like to STRANGLE you with my bare hands.
Instead I will pray for your soul. But ALL SINNERS
BURN IN HELL. Stay away from my boys!

Sincerely,
A Concerned Neighbor

I picked up another note, smoothed it out, and brought it to
the light. Same thing: *Dirty Homo. Filthy Swear Word. Burn in Hell.*
I got another note and brought it to the light.
Filthy this. Dirty that. Burn in Hell.
Before I read another, I unplugged the standing lamp and
carried it to the circle of crumpled letters, so I didn't have to
keep going back and forth with the pages. There was an outlet
on the far side of the foosball table. I knelt to plug the cord,
fumbling in the dark to get the prongs in, all the while with that
taste in my mouth, copper, iron, something else—
When I lit up the dark corner I realized (and smelled) what
that dummy was. That dummy wasn't a dummy. That dummy
was Robbie Morton. And it wasn't Robbie Morton's face that
was missing. It was the back of Robbie's head. He was facing the
corner with his back to me and his body wrapped in Dee-dee's
hippie shawl. I tripped on the gun at his side, screamed, and ran
upstairs.

FOURTEEN

My scream broke Dee-dee's trance.

She was still sitting motionless at the kitchen table by last night's pizza. When I ran up screaming she started screaming too and would not stop. She screamed through my phone call to the operator and screamed through my call to the police. Covering the phone and hollering Dee-dee stop screaming didn't help. She was stuck in a scream. I could hardly hear the policeman ask, name, address, are you certain he's dead, check for a pulse, the ambulance is on the way, etcetera.

Dee-dee screamed right through my stumble back downstairs to make sure Robbie was dead (yes horribly so with his brains blown out and pieces of his skull all over the nice clean basement) and when I got off the phone we both screamed right through as we hid the drugs (like all drug-taking teenagers will do even in dire emergencies) and screamed as we rushed to find the screwdriver from the garage (not there) and screamed as we searched the pencil drawer (there the screwdriver was among the rulers, rubber bands, and paper clips) and screamed as we unscrewed the closet panel and stuffed in her cigar box and screamed as we put the liqueur back in the liquor cabinet and aired out her room and screamed as we ran screaming with our unbrushed teeth, uncombed hair, and bare feet from that cursed house.

We ran screaming up Highlook Drive to the meadow beyond and tumbled screaming into the haunted Ford truck. We sat screaming in the rising dust and mouse droppings on the musty seat springs of that old truck, clutching each other and screaming till our throats wore out like old doors no one used anymore swinging on rusty hinges, screek-screek, our screams keened till our voices fell to rust and we both fell asleep screaming.

We didn't move or speak till Holly found us in late afternoon. The sun was pouring in and we were sweating but our skin was cold. We moved like old ladies trying to get out of that truck. Holly had to pry us apart, as if Dee-dee and I had died in there long ago from some tragic accident.

FIFTEEN

We were both questioned by the police. We were questioned separately and questioned together. We were questioned and questioned and questioned some more. Was there anyone else in the house? A friend of yours? A friend of Robbie's? Or some stranger? Did you give Robbie drugs? Was Robbie doing drugs with a friend? Did you force drugs on Robbie? Did you hear the gunshot? Did you give him the gun? Did you know about the gun? Did you know Robbie was feeling suicidal?

No there was no one else in the house. No we didn't give Robbie drugs. No we didn't hear the gunshot. No we didn't know he had a gun. No we didn't know Robbie was feeling suicidal. Robbie was the same as usual. Maybe he was crying again and maybe he left his pizza slices, but he was a moody boy. And NO WE DIDN'T KNOW HE WAS GOING TO PUT A GUN TO HIS HEAD AND BLOW HIS BRAINS OUT.

And we didn't know about the letters. Well not about the ones to Robbie. We never showed those letters to the cops. And we never told them about our time travel, or girl-kissing, or magic spells, or they'd think we were Crazy Lezbo Witches and put us in the blender. Or throw us in jail for MAIL THEFT.

We just hunched over, wiped our noses, and shook our heads. I shrugged a lot. I wasn't sure how Dee-dee felt but I was completely numb, like the dentist had stuck my whole body with

Novocain.

Finally the cops stopped questioning us and lecturing us and let us go home. I crawled into bed and dreamed of Robbie wrapped in Dee-dee's shawl with the back of his head missing, but he wasn't in Morton's basement. He was in a small cave hunched over like some old man chanting in ancient Egyptian. Robbie's chants filled my dreams and I woke with my mouth tasting like green mush in the overflowing toilets of Sleepland.

"You have to go to school."

Next morning Dad sat at the head of the table with his smoke rising and his hand round a coffee cup, "If you don't go today it'll be that much harder tomorrow."

Mom didn't say anything, just took a bite of raisin toast and turned the newspaper, her mouth shut like a scar.

Dad went to shave with the bathroom door cracked, the hot water running, and the scent of Old Spice, then walked to the front hall with a bit of bloody toilet paper stuck to his chin, picked up his briefcase, and went out the door.

"Mom?"

Mom just looked at me with her jaw chewing, and I knew I had to go to my first day at Highlook Junior High after Robbie Morton killed himself.

At first everyone was like eggshells. At the bus stop Holly was silent. Melody made her mouth into a tight line. A circle opened around me. Dee-dee didn't come to school that day. The bus came. I got on. No one sat with me. I looked out the window. The other kids didn't turn their heads and stare at me, and didn't whisper *shame on you*, but I knew they were looking at me through the backs of their heads and thinking *shame on you*, like my sixth grade field trip when I dropped my burger bag out the window with a state trooper driving right behind and the whole bus filled with susurrations of *litterbug*.

No one was saying *you did it, it's your fault*, but everyone was thinking YOU DID IT, IT'S YOUR FAULT, you were in the Morton house when Robbie put that gun to his head. Bet you were high on grass, bet you were high on LSD, bet you had your tongue down Dee-dee Morton's throat in a lesbian orgy and that's why Robbie Morton killed himself.

And in classes, in the halls, and at my locker, everyone was thinking, it's your fault. Even my good friend Stringbean wouldn't talk to me in school.

Dee-dee came to the bus stop next week.

All her lights had gone out.

I stood by her. A circle opened around us. The bus came. We got on. Dee-dee and I sat together. I felt everyone thinking you both did it, with your tongues down each other's throats.

Then Dee-dee stopped riding the school bus. And stopped talking to me. And stopped dropping by. And didn't call. Or pick up the phone.

"Give her time," Mom said.

I gave her time. I gave her a week. Then two.

And I wasn't invited to the funeral.

"They didn't have a funeral," Mom said. "Well, they had a funeral, but no one was invited. No one but immediate family."

Immediate family?

What did that mean? I was the one who time traveled with Dee-dee. I was the one with the invisible river of electricity running from my body to hers. I was the one who kissed her all over until she exploded. If I wasn't immediate, who was?

After three long weeks I screwed my courage to the sticking place and walked up the slope towards Dee-dee's olive green split-level. I stood staring at the low rock wall alongside her front door where the stone sparkles caught the sun. The sun wasn't shining that day, but I could see where the flecks would catch if it were shining. I took heart in those flecks and rang the bell.

She didn't come on the first ring. Or the second. On the third ring, I leaned on the bell with all my heart bursting. I needed to see Dee-dee, needed to feel the fine hairs on her arms, maybe get a whiff of her scent, maybe get sucked in her embrace, dragged up to her room and drowned on her bed with our legs entangled in silent ecstasy.

She answered on the fifth ring. Her lips were chapped. Her nose was red. She hugged a pale pink sweater to her chest, so faded it looked dirty, with tiny pearl-beads forming dumb flowers. I'd never seen that sweater before.

Where was her hippie shawl?

Oh right.

Maybe that pink sweater was her mom's. Maybe she'd just tugged it on to answer the door. Maybe she had nothing on under but bare skin and warm breasts—

And why couldn't I open my mouth?

I opened my mouth. Nothing came out.

I knew there were words down in my cold insides, words like good soldiers marching. *Dee-dee I love you. Dee-dee I need you. Dee-dee I'm sorry. Dee-dee you lit a fire in me that's going to burn down the whole neighborhood.*

I knew this was one of those moments when it was okay for one girl to put her arm around another. I was sure of that. I took a breath, stepped forward, and lifted my arm.

She shrank from me, backed inside, and shut the door.

I stared at the flecked rocks. Was it my fault? That last sleepover? Robbie staring out the kitchen window at nothing? Were there words floating out there? Hateful words? *Dirty Homo? Filthy Faggot? Burn in Hell?* Those poison notes.

Who'd write such things?

After Dee-dee shut the door I stood staring at the doorbell for a long time wishing she'd come back out crying with tears streaming down her face so I could take her in my arms and kiss her pain away and we could walk arm in arm down to the lake and wade into the cold and sit together in the freezing wet and drown ourselves before the lake froze. The lake wouldn't freeze for another month. We still had time to plan our perfect death. I pressed the bell again. No answer. I stood there as the shadows lengthened, knowing Mrs. Green and the other neighbors were peeking through their curtains. Let them peek. Their staring wouldn't move me. I'd stay at Dee-dee's door till the sun set and night fell and the stars shone. I'd stay till the leaves turned and jack-o-lanterns glowed and White Rock froze solid. Only one thing got me away from Dee-dee's house that day. One thing only.

SIXTEEN

To carve a perfect chalk canoe.

I found the exacto knife in the art supply drawer, picked up a fresh chalk from the blackboard, sat at my old place at the dining room table and started carving.

Scritch-scratch, I would not stop—

Soon I had a pile of brokens higher than any previous pile in our dining room. "Move that pile to your room," Mom said. I stuffed all the canoes in my pillowcase and dumped them on my closet floor, all my brokens with their dots of blood, for it was my room now, my room and my room only after years of sharing with my sisters, my room and my closet covered in bloody little canoes and my hands filling with tiny cuts and my days filling again with the music the chalk made as I stroked my fingers through, tink-tink, and I didn't care if the knife slipped and wounds opened like tiny mouths saying *carve a perfect one!* I listened to those tiny mouths and each time I started a fresh stick I thought *the next shall be perfect.* And they always broke. The knife slipped and pierced my skin and never did I wipe the blood and never did I bandage the cuts and never did I sweep the dust. I carved even in sleep, and with each perfect fresh stick in my dreams my heart opened like a flower and closed again as the chalk broke and my hopes of ever carving a perfect chalk canoe flowed further and further away.

I was pursuing perfection.

Perfection with canoes but nothing else. In junior high my grades dropped to C's then D's. I no longer brought books home. I killed flies and smeared them on my wall. When I didn't have to be in school or helping with supper I was under the covers trying to die or carving chalk canoes. After school I carved in front of the TV with Love Boat, Mike Douglas, Johnny Carson, and in school my fingers itched to get carving again as the words on the pages of Social Studies and the numbers of Algebra and the sounds coming from the teachers' mouths and the screak of their blackboard chalk all turned into the scritch-scratch of my knife on each canoe as I ruined it.

I could still taste and smell Dee-dee, and if I closed my eyes and touched my arm I could pretend it was her. In the privacy of my room I spit in my fingers, spread my legs, and touched myself with pictures in my head of a boy on the dock touching my bikini, then Dee-dee over me, her woman-weight, woman breasts, and woman-scent, as I exploded in my private darkness.

But that hurt too. I'd see Dee-dee, then I'd see the corpse in the dark corner of her basement. No, that's not a body. That's a dummy made by Robbie and Zipper. No that's not a dummy made by Robbie and Zipper. That's Robbie Morton with the back of his head blown off.

Where had Zipper Zupinski been that night? Why hadn't he slept over with Robbie? Zipper wasn't talking. And the gun, where had that come from? The gun, I later learned, came from Mr. Zupinski. He kept it in a locked case, and Robbie and Zipper found the key and messed with it on the sly.

And what about the Poison Pens? Who wrote those evil letters? Did they feel what I felt? Guilt and remorse, like the long-buried dead? All those questions buzzed in my head as I carved away. With my hands busy, up came the pictures—Dee-dee, her mouth, Robbie, his stone-face, Zipper, his red smile—as the canoes broke and broke. With each canoe, up came a smell, sound, or picture. I'd feel Dee-dee near, hear her throaty whisper, *I am crazy-mad about you Cat*, feel her hands on my nipples, then I'd leave my body as my hands kept carving away at the ever-breaking canoe.

I'm slow.

It takes time for me to put two and two together. I didn't put two and two together till I went back to Mr. Swanson's sixth grade room. By then my junior high teachers had given up on me. Well they never tried. Why should they? They didn't know me. But word got down to Mr. Swanson that his favorite weirdo straight A student from last year was failing at Highlook Junior High, so he sent a note.

Come see me after school.

I went reluctantly.

Mr. Swanson was a big guy from the Iron Range, square torso, broad shoulders, and hips so narrow he could barely keep his pants up. Mr. Swanson didn't ask how I was I feeling, didn't say I should get over what happened, and didn't whisper, did you drug Robbie?

He just put me to work scoring papers for his English class. A stack of real-life stories. He told me mark for misspelling and grammar, since he knew I had a gift for both.

Those kids were suffering—worse than I. They didn't know how to spell *murdur* or *tresspass* and they had shitty lives. Gilly Beaumont's mom had severe arthritis. Bonnie White's grandma wore diapers. Vince Keller's dad died in a car crash. Harold Colby's brother beat him up. Gloria Dickerson's sister drowned in Big Snake. Timmy Wheeler's brother died in Vietnam. All those kids had hidden heartaches.

One girl didn't want to be alone with her dad. Another had a mom who shoplifted. Another kid had a mom who made them pray all the time, not just at supper, but in the morning and afternoon and at night in front of the TV. Every day they had to get down on their knees and ask for forgiveness of their sins, and if they hadn't sinned that day, they had to make up sins or their mom would smack them.

I sat in Mr. Swanson's empty classroom with that praying kid's paper shaking in my hands—like Dee-dee's hands shook with the first yellowed note.

This paper was written by Flipper Zupinski.

Zipper's little brother.

It was typed on translucent onionskin. The words *morning* and *night* and *forgiveness* all had missing tails on the lower case g.

I remembered back to that horrible sleepover morning.

Dee-dee had sobbed between screams, we have to hide them Cat, we have to hide those letters, Robbie wouldn't want anyone to read them. She meant the awful Poison Pens, and I didn't disagree, not out loud, not after she'd just lost her brother, but she was dead wrong. If Robbie hadn't wanted anyone to read the letters he wouldn't have blown his brains out with them laid in a circle around him. He wanted people to see that sticks and stones break bones and nasty words break souls and splatter them all over the basement. But I wasn't at that moment thinking clearly, so I went down to the basement for a third time. Facing that corpse for a third time and gathering up those hateful letters with the poor back of Robbie's skull staring at me wasn't the hardest part. The hardest part was lying later when the cops asked did you find a suicide note of any kind, written on a scrap of paper or torn from a magazine or anything? Dee-dee and I lied and said no. It was a lie because those Poison Pens were as good as twelve suicide notes. Need a good reason to kill yourself? Here's a dozen.

We stuffed those Poison Pens in the orange Kinney shoe box and put the box behind that wooden panel in Dee-dee's closet with all the yellowed letters.

Now I wanted those Poison Pens back. I wanted to hold them in my hands and study them, for if there were Poison Pens to Robbie and Tammy and Dee-dee, perhaps there were others.

Sure enough, in the very next kid's paper.

Somebody sent a nasty letter to my mom.

In another: *Somebody wrote my sister was a dirty whore.*

And a third: *Dad burnt a bad letter in our barbeque.*

Whatever the Poison Pen felt after Robbie's death, it didn't stop them. They were still writing venom and stuffing it in our mailboxes. And with Flipper's paper shaking in my hands, I wished we hadn't lied to the cops about those Poison Pens.

For how would anyone stop them now? If Robbie's death didn't stop them, what would?

If Dee-dee would meet with me, we could figure out what to do with this important clue.

I could imagine what Dee-dee would do. She'd do just what I didn't expect her to. Instead of saying, that lower case g means the Poison Pens came from the Zupinskis' house, she'd whisper, do not jump to conclusions Cat. That is the first rule of solving mysteries. It could be anyone. Flipper could have typed his paper at the Carters', or the bratty twins'. The Poison Pen could be the grandma, or the babysitter, or old Mrs. Green. It could be a window peeper crawling in to type them. Surely the Poison Pen would not be so obvious as to use their very own typewriter! Do not make hasty assumptions, Cat.

That's what Dee-dee would say.

Do not jump to conclusions.

Perhaps it is not the obvious.

No perhaps it is not the obvious. Perhaps it's not the lady with the red grin who bikes through our neighborhood with the ding-ding of her bell and her bike seat swallowed by her big rear end and her basket stuffed with neighborhood flyers about City Council Meetings and Christmas Caroling and Easter Egg Hunts and Stockyard Days Parades with Bible tracts tucked underneath about *Life, Death, and Eternal Sin.* Perhaps it's not her with her binoculars stuck to her picture window spying on my sister and shaming her, and, I later learn, shaming nearly everyone in White Rock. No, perhaps it's not her who makes her boys kneel and pray in front of the TV and make up sins so she has something to forgive them for. Perhaps not. Or perhaps we were all dirty sinners, all of us, drowning in sin.

SEVENTEEN

Dee-dee left the next week. A sign went up in her yard.

FOR SALE
BEAUMONT REALTY
No Place Like Home

The cursed house was for sale. I heard Dee-dee was moving to the orange brick apartment up the curve, a faux colonial where the poor White Rockers lived, the newlyweds, hippies, and young ladies just leaving home.

Downhill, that's where Dee-dee and her mom were heading when they moved up the slope, and they left a bunch of stuff against the back of their house under an old army tarp.

That Saturday I saw the moving truck in their driveway and walked up pretending to look for the cat, "Here kitty." Mrs. Morton was in the driveway with Dee-dee's Aunt Cindy loading stuff in the back, but I saw no sign of Dee-dee.

Was she inside dismantling her bedroom? Where would she put all her dangling things, the brass bells, bones-on-a-string, dried flowers, and Barbie dolls trapped in fisherman's nets?

If she took them down, they'd get all tangled, and she'd have to cut the whole mess apart. What about the dead bat tacked to the wall? It would crumble to dust at her touch, like her old tomes of spells. And what would she do with all our yellowed letters? And the Poison Pens? Would she leave them in her closet to molder behind the wooden panel? I imagined mice back there chewing all the letters into infinitesimal bits.

I still had her Egyptian Book of the Dead. And her straw sunhat. She'd forgotten the hat down at our beach, and she didn't need it now, with the cold nights and turning leaves. I put the hat up on my closet shelf where it could watch over my sea of broken chalk canoes.

"Here kitty," I called the morning of the moving truck, but saw no sign of Dee-dee. I went back after the truck was gone and tried to look in the windows, but I felt Mrs. Green behind her drapes, and I was tired of the stares and whispers. I'd go back later and lift that tarp to see what they'd left behind. For that I needed the cover of darkness.

Next Saturday we played Bars Down.

The leaves were falling, the cold was numbing, and all the neighbor kids gathered in our street. The bratty twins' front door was base, a broomstick was the bar, and I ran and hid by the shrubbery behind Dee-dee's.

No one would go there.

But the cute boy showed up and hid with me. We sat silently side-by-side in the setting sun, just the cute boy and I, sweaty from running, dirty from crawling, panting with the danger of capture. I imagined in a moment the cute boy would put his hand on my knee. Then his hand would slide up my thigh. Then his hand would clasp my breast. Then his lips would meet mine in a kiss—

Then his mom called him home for supper.

Alone, with a fire burning between my legs and night falling on the backs of the houses, I crept towards the army tarp. I could just see the black rectangles of the Morton windows, the dark tarp, and the hump of whatever lay under.

Feeling beneath, I fingered a stick of wood, a sliding stack of magazines, a camp stool—

My hand touched something satiny, hard and slippery.

A deep voice bellowed, "Hey you!"

A stripe of light fell on the next lawn.

"Get away from there!"

I tripped backwards, ran in a crouch, and tore home.

As I lay in bed that night. I knew with my fairy-tale brain raised on holes in trees leading to underworlds of trolls and piles of gold and heads lopped off and pricked fingers with blood dripping and men turning into beasts and beasts turning back into men, I knew like my fingers knew the newly hairy place between my legs, knew by the feel of the thing under all that discarded stuff what it was under that army tarp. It was the abandoned mummy. Dee-dee had left it behind. Just like she'd left me.

That night I dreamed of the mummy coming to life, throwing off his tarp and walking the neighborhood like a skinny Frankenstein monster, arms out, heart aching in loneliness and the dread of being left.

I tried to catch the mummy in my dream, tried to take him in my arms and comfort him. I chased him all over the neighborhood, through the backyards, by the haunted Ford truck, past the low rock wall of the old ice house foundation, and through the brambles and stickers on the other side of the lake. I finally caught him by the storm sewer, just before he crawled into its mouth of oblivion. But once he was finally in my arms, his tears burned my skin like sulfuric acid, his moans tore my eardrums, and his body crumbled at my touch—to nothing. I woke up sobbing, with an ache in my chest like a stone.

EIGHTEEN

"So, what're you gonna be, Cat?"

Stringbean was hovering over me chomping Hubba Bubba as I sat carving in the dining room.

"Huh, Cat? What?"

I wasn't going to be anything. When you've lain beside a genuine mummy and held a naked girl in your arms and seen the back of a head blown off, what did you care about plastic masks, fake blood, and Butterfingers?

"I was gonna be a mummy," Stringbean chomped, "but Zipper said he's gonna be. But I thought of it first. And Zipper's using toilet paper. Toilet paper won't work! Toilet paper is white! Mummies aren't white. I have rags, Cat. To steep in coffee. Like a real mummy."

I kept my mouth shut.

Stringbean knew nothing of the real mummy.

"You gonna be a witch again, Cat? Or Cleopatra?"

Not Cleopatra!

Nefertiti, like the beautiful bust in the history books.

If I were going, I would go as Nefertiti, leave my old self behind, and be a mysterious beauty with black round my eyes, like Theda Bara glaring from the poster at Dee-dee's.

Abandon Hope All Yee Who Look At Me.

But I wasn't going trick-or-treating.

I had canoes to carve.

Stringbean went on about how we'd egg mailboxes, toilet-paper trees, and scare little kids, then she blew a big bubble.

POP! went her bubble.

SNAP! The canoe broke in my hands.

In the apple barrel, I found Tammy's black wig and beaded headdress, and in my underwear drawer there was Dee-dee's white nightgown. I hadn't worn the nightgown since our time-travel night. It seemed dangerous. I figured some spell was still attached to it, and if I put it on I'd get slipped back to the snow-covered Voyageur, or a Viking slave ship, or the black hole of infinity. But I took that risk for Halloween.

After supper I set down the exacto knife, brushed off the chalk dust and opened my underwear drawer.

There was the nightgown with the shoulder rip from that night, torn on a thorny branch by the frowning church. Dee-dee had said, rip it to shreds when we are done, Cat!

I could never shred this nightgown.

I held the thin cotton to my nose, closed my eyes and slid it on, ready to be sucked back—

Nothing happened.

So I painted my eyes, put on the wig, and bobby-pinned the headdress. In the mirror I looked a real beauty, Queen Nefertiti, with clothes layered under to keep out the cold. I'd keep a solemn face all night.

Stringbean came to the door as a lean werewolf, with fake-fur sideburns, a brown-painted nose, and her dad's yellow-plaid blazer smeared with ketchup.

She roared as she stepped in, "Rhaaa!"

Spit came stringing from her plastic teeth.

"Yuck, Stringbean!"

She opened her pillowcase with a wink to reveal a flashlight, three rolls of toilet paper, and a carton of eggs, and out the door we went.

Kids swarmed all over our street. The bratty twins were vampires, all the Blakes were stumbling zombies, Flipper Zupinski was a pirate.

Mr. Anderson frowned down at us with his rake, saying, aren't you kids a little old for trick-or-treating?

We ignored him, went up his steps and rang the bell.

Mrs. Anderson opened the door smiling in her square-dance petticoats, dropped two Baby Ruths in our pillowcases, and on we ran to the next house. With all the grinning jack-o-lanterns, yelping kids, throngs of Draculas, Batmans, and cheerful moms with bowlfuls of Sweet Tarts, Red Hots, and Three Musketeers, my dragging despair got left behind.

I had to trot to keep up with Stringbean, her long legs traversing the yards. We cut right through, and clumsy me, I tripped over shrubs, walked into trees, and stumbled over stuffed dummies by hidden speakers booming in the voice of the dead.

I was catching my breath by Dee-dee's when the idea hit. I'd already taken part in Stringbean's nasty acts. I'd broken eggs in mailboxes, thrown toilet paper into trees, and scared little kids. I figured Stringbean could help me hatch an evil plan of my own. Well not evil. Dangerous. And scary.

Dee-dee's house stood with the FOR SALE sign. No buyers. Still cursed.

Stringbean was clutching her flashlight. In the dark she was never without it.

"Stringbean," I said, "there's something I need to see."

Before she could ask what, I added, "But it's spooky. And dangerous. We'd be risking our lives."

That would get her.

"Where is it?" she asked. "Let's go!"

"Shh."

I put my finger to my lips. My stomach dropped. Halloween tricks were one thing, but Dee-dee's house was the site of a real-life tragedy. I touched the werewolf hair on Stringbean's chest, lowered my voice, and made my Nefertiti face expressionless.

The headdress jangled as I shook my head.

"Stringbean, we have to get serious."

Three little kids galloped by giggling, then went quiet and ran silently past Dee-dee's. Only new kids who knew no better walked on that lawn.

Stringbean's face had gone white.

I put my lips to her hairy ear.

"You cannot tell anyone about this, Stringbean. You cannot tell anyone we went in Morton's yard. And you cannot tell anyone we lifted the tarp. And you cannot tell anyone what we find under. Never ever."

All the kids knew about that tarp. I'd heard the whispered jokes on the school bus as it went past the cursed house. Whispers of, bet Robbie Morton's buried under there, bet they couldn't give him a church burial 'cause he committed suicide.

We entered Dee-dee's backyard. The windows were dead-blank. I knew what was behind every pane. There was the kitchen window where Dee-dee and I ate Cap'n Crunch. There was Dee-dee's bedroom window where all the rivers of the world, all the mouths of the rivers and streams and rivulets flowed together and dashed, tumbled, and roared into waterfalls that led to the sea when Dee-dee kissed me. And there was the bathroom where I washed Robbie Morton's brains from my hands.

The army tarp was disturbed. Had the mummy escaped? Had it come to life as the boy with cobalt-blue eyes? Was he walking the neighborhood now, chanting in ancient Egyptian? Or maybe a dog ran off with a leg. Or some bigger kid, like sassy Melody, sniffed the mummy out with her sassy sniffer and said oh what a perfect thing to scare Stringbean and her dumb friend Cat with, scare them out of their skins!

I reached under the tarp. Beneath the camp stool, damp magazines and boxes, I felt something hard going soft.

"Stringbean," I whispered, "get your flashlight in here, but keep it low."

Crouching in the damp leaves, Stringbean turned on the Eveready, shielding the beam with her dinner-plate hands.

"Ready?"

"Ready!"

I threw back the tarp.

There it was. Under the camp stool. Silent, sober, regal.

The mummy.

Stringbean laughed.

"Ha! Funny one, Cat McCloud! Funny one! Ah!"

She leapt back, dropping the flashlight. The beam fell on the far shrubbery. "Very funny," she hissed. "Ha!" She rolled on the ground, her pillowcase abandoned. "Ha!" Tears of horrified laughter smeared her wolf-face.

I rushed to quiet her. She lurched up and tackled me, rolling me to Morton's dead lawn, pinning my arms, knocking off my headdress and wig. With my arms pinned and her handsome face over me, Stringbean spit in my mouth. My open mouth.

I spit back.

"Hey!"

A stripe of light fell from the neighbor's backdoor.

"You kids! Get away from there!"

Stringbean and I rolled belly-to-belly into the thorny shrubs.

She whispered through plastic teeth with her hot tears falling on my Nefertiti cheeks, "How could you, Cat? That's not even funny! That's the worst thing anyone has ever done to me! Worse than when Melody made me drink a blenderized toad. You are so mean, Cat! I didn't know that about you! I never knew you could be so MEAN!"

"Shh!"

The neighbor was still at his screen door.

Stringbean lowered her voice but kept blubbering.

"How could you, Cat?"

Three more werewolf tears fell on my lip. Her plastic teeth fell out. In spite of everything, the neighbor, the thorny bushes, and Stringbean's tears, a fire started in my hips.

I wiped her tears from my face. A line of snot descended from her nose. I rolled away just in time, dashed from the bushes, tore from the Morton backyard and into the pool of streetlight.

My hands were bleeding, and Tammy's wig and headdress were in the cursed yard, along with Stringbean's teeth. I heard Stringbean still there, her breath catching on sobs.

I bit my lip. I'd have to crawl back to retrieve the headdress and wig or Tammy would kill me. Especially if I lost them in that yard. I headed for the shadows between houses.

Safely back in my room, I explained it all to Stringbean. Well not all. Not how Dee-dee and I got entangled naked together. I wouldn't talk of that, or our time travel. But I told Stringbean about the mummy—all I knew.

I told her no, I wasn't trying to scare her out of her skin with a realistic replica of a corpse to make her think we'd uncovered the body of poor Robbie.

"I would never do that to you, Stringbean!"

She sniffed, peeling bits of fake fur from her cheeks and lining them up on my bed like sleeping gerbils.

"I would never, ever do that to you."

I was crying too, at the shock of Stringbean's shock. Her tackle had loosened something in me. Sharing anything after the tragedy of Robbie broke me open. I kept repeating, "I would never do that to you, Stringbean, and never do that to the memory of Robbie."

I wiped my nose. *The memory of Robbie?*

What had I ever done for Robbie? I just sat silent in Mr. Swanson's sixth grade as tears rolled down Robbie's cheeks and kids teased him. I never tapped his shoulder and asked, why are you crying, Robbie? Or, what's the matter, Robbie? Or, please stop crying Robbie. And what had I done that sleepover night when he turned to white stone? Nothing. Just ate his pizza.

I sighed.

Stringbean was staring at our pillowcases with her mouth open. Her plastic teeth were in Dee-dee's yard. Our candy was in two piles on my bed. The piles weren't nearly as big as last Halloween's. I read her mind.

"Wanna go back out?"

She nodded.

We took our empty pillowcases back out as we were, toothless Werewolf and tear-stained Nefertiti.

Most of the kids were in, except the big ones slinking towards Dead End Woods or to wild parties on Big Snake.

After filling our pillowcases, we went back to the mummy, this time quietly. We'd planned to wrap the body in the tarp and take it to my house. Then what? We'd figure that out when we got there. For now we needed to get that mummy out of the damp. Surely it would mildew under that tarp, then flower with mold, then bring down all the curses from *The Book of the Dead*.

Let not my flesh rot.

Let not my limbs mildew.

Let not my body flower with the grave!

We crept towards the tarp on tiptoe. No flashlight this time. We needed the cover of darkness. Oh-so-slowly we moved the camp stool. Oh-so-gently we parted the junk. Oh-so-tenderly we began to move the mummy.

"It stinks!" Stringbean whispered.

"No it doesn't."

Stringbean sniffed. "What now?"

"Roll it up in the tarp."

"Okay."

"I'll take the shoulders. You take the feet. On three."

Stringbean nodded. In the dark, the remains of her werewolf makeup resembled a disintegrating zombie.

"One, two, three."

We rolled the mummy.

"Gently."

We managed to roll it thrice, its shoulders oh-so-scrawny.

"Ready to lift and carry?"

"Yes."

"One, two—"

"What're you kids doing?"

The stripe of light again from the neighbor's—

"Run!"

Holding the tarped mummy horizontally, we side-stepped into the shadows on the far side of Dee-dee's. Huffing there, we heard the neighbor burp, then silence. Finally he shut his door, murmuring, "Damn kids."

Stringbean gave a lurch.

"Wait."

In the dark I counted to fifty.

"Okay."

We tiptoed into the street. No big kids in sight.

A dark cat ran past.

"Whoa."

We nearly dropped our bundle.

The streetlight cast the mummy's shadow momentarily on the asphalt. Seven more houses and we'd be home. What then? In the back door? Or the front? Or down to the lake? Where to hide the bundle?

"BOO!"

Holly and Melody leapt out from behind Mrs. Green's.

Stringbean dropped her end.

We inadvertently up-righted the tarped mummy.

Holly bellowed in her deep dad-voice, "Hey you!"

Melody sassed, "Ga-erls! What you doing out so late!? Huh?"

They were drunk, and dressed like Raggedy Anne and Andy, with red yarn hair, red-circle cheeks, and blood-shot eyes. They'd come from some party up the street.

Melody put her hands on her hips.

"What are you supposed to be? Huh? Bums? Girl bum? Boy bum? Ha. Trick or treat. Who's that?"

She gestured towards the tarped mummy. "Hell-o."

She smacked it with the back of her hand. "You."

She smacked again. "Who're you 'spozed to be. Huh?"

I drew the tarped mummy back.

"Shy, are you?" Melody stank of wine. "Who's in there, ga-erls? Who's your skinny little friend? Why are you hiding, huh? Come over here. Let me see."

Holly wavered behind, too drunk to speak.

I sighed. In situations like this, it's best to tell the truth.

"It's a mummy," I said. "An ancient Egyptian mummy. A three thousand year old mummy preserved with great care by first pulverizing the brain, then drawing it out through the nose with a long spoon in a process called excerebration—"

"Shut up, smarty-pants!" Melody slapped it again.

I stepped back.

Melody stepped forward.

"Doesn't look like a muh-mummy to me," she slurred.

Swack!

"Looks like a skinny kid wrapped in a tarp."

Swack!

"Come out, skinny kid!"

SWACK!

"I'm a mummy!" I said in the voice of death—

"A real mummy!"

I drew the tarp from its head, revealing the crusty skull.

"And if you mock me, I SHALL CURSE YOU TO HELL!"

Melody stumbled back with a gasp.

Holly blinked.

The mummy's head fell to the street.

It rocked on the asphalt, to and fro, as Melody screamed, grabbed Holly, and lurched back to the drunken party.

By the time they disappeared between houses, the head had stopped rocking.

Stringbean stared down at it.

"Here," I said, passing the headless body to her.

Stringbean held the wrapped torso, light as a bundle of sticks, upright with her long fingers.

I knelt by the skin-covered skull, looked into the sunken eyeholes, and touched the grimacing lips.

"Oh you, poor you."

I picked the head up tenderly and carried it home.

Stringbean followed.

NINETEEN

"Masking tape won't work," Stringbean said. "Do you have any duck tape?"

I shrugged.

The headless mummy was safe for now on my bedroom floor, out of sight on the far side of my four-poster.

Stringbean and I knelt beside him.

Mom was asleep, Dad was snoring on the living room floor, and Holly was off at her drunken party.

"I don't think—"

I wasn't able to finish my sentence. Somehow duct tape didn't seem right. Duct tape was of the twentieth century. What would a mummy-maker mend a mummy with? Not duct tape. Even if they had duct tape back then, I don't think they'd use it to reattach a head. The charms and chants from Dee-dee's Book of the Dead rang through me:

Let not my arms be cut off.

Let not my feet be lost.

Let not my head be separated from my body!

What could we use to reattach the head? Something gelatinous, like oatmeal. Something fibrous, like tree bark. Something from mother nature, like bacon. Chicken skin! Leather was skin! Meat was muscle! Stringbean and I would bike to Howie's Butcher Shop and buy steak. There wasn't much muscle around the mummy's neck. We'd need just a few strips, like the meat we sizzled in the fondue-pot over the tiny burner on special occasions. How I loved that meat sizzling in oil! How I loved to eat it bloody! Fondue meat would be perfect.

We returned the tarp to Dee-dee's backyard and dried the meat for the mummy-repair using two methods: Holly's hair dryer and iodized salt. I salted steak strips till they dried into jerky after carefully wrapping and pinning them with a toothpick in muscular weavings over the vertebrae, the atlas and axis, supporting the globe of the head. I'd studied anatomy. I knew the complexity. I carefully wove and wrapped. My excellent plan!

To further guarantee the head was firm upon the body, I stripped raw skin from a chicken and wrapped that round using the same methods. Genius! Before all the delicate weaving, Stringbean and I pressed a wad of Strawberry Hubba Bubba Bubble Gum between the vertebrae for adhesion. We did this delicate operation over the next week. Mom never went in my room anyway, but just in case, I took three beach towels and covered the mummy. It was November. Nobody needed those beach towels till next June.

Once the mummy's head was securely attached, I got another brilliant idea. I'd store it in my closet. After getting more salt from Red Owl, I stuffed all my chalk canoes into my pillowcase, put the mummy on my closet floor, then poured thirty canisters of salt over the dried corpse. As salt poured into his mouth and nostrils, I felt queasy about suffocating him, but he had to be preserved. He'd gotten damp and moldy behind Dee-dee's. The salt whispered down from the silvery spouts, salty snowbanks covered my mummy, then I covered the salt with broken chalk canoes. Tink, they made their little sound as they blanketed him. In case Mom (or god forbid Holly) ever went in my closet, my usual pile of brokens was all they'd see.

Then came Thanksgiving with my little nieces and nephews romping through, giggling, galloping into my room, falling into my closet and running their hands through my chalk canoes. Just in time I shooed them out.

Before the wee ones converged again at Christmas, I put a silent movie poster on my door. I couldn't find Theda Bara like Dee-dee's, but found the Frankenstein monster with his arms out stiff and threatening, and wrote below in dripping tempera, *STAY OUT OR DIE!*

After Christmas three snowstorms locked us in till spring, and all winter long, I tried to carve a perfect chalk canoe, and drew pictures on my bedroom walls of the mummy, Dee-dee as a mermaid, and our time-travel night.

I still had the thorn in my jewelry box, and the scars on my arms from the mosquito bites, along with the memory of that Voyageur covered in snow with his pouch of statuettes.

While carving I'd find myself back in that bitter cold I didn't feel, staring down at that vomiting Voyageur in the white and black woods so long ago, with French sounds coming out his grizzled mouth, je suis, la petite fleur, mon amour.

Paging through Mom's art history books, I discovered two lithographs like those the Voyageur had cooed over. The Fat Lady, with her huge belly and breasts, was just like a twenty-seven thousand year old stone carving called *Venus of Willendorf*. And the Lion Man was like the thirty thousand year old mammoth-tusk carving called *the Lion Man of Hohlenstein-Stadel*. On my bedroom wall I drew those ancient carvings surrounded by Egyptian hieroglyphs, with my sketch of Dee-dee hovering over, her breasts floating, scales twinkling, mermaid hair encircling all.

Dee-dee's house still hadn't sold. The FOR SALE sign got covered with snow. No one shoveled the driveway. The tarp was hidden by white drifts. We lucked out, Stringbean said, to get that mummy out when we did.

Yes we lucked out. Now the mummy was safe under my pile of broken chalk canoes, like the fish under the ice of Little Rose. Mr. Anderson put his ice house out. So did the Carters, Blakes, and Zupinskis. They were all out in their little houses on the flat ice on the long winter nights, holding a pole and staring down into their private holes waiting for a nibble, keeping warm with hot chocolate or booze, catching crappies and northerns, with perhaps a snapping turtle nosing up to the hole with its sharp beak and white-lidded eyes, then jerking forward, quick as lightning, to bite off a finger.

Stringbean ice-fished too, but not me. I had better things to do. Like forget about Dee-dee. As the ice creaked in the long nights with the fishers hunched over their holes and the Poison Pen hunched over the typewriter, my mummy lay hidden under all those broken chalk canoes in my closet, and I carved chalk canoe after broken chalk canoe, dreaming of the day when I could set that mummy free.

TWENTY

Dee-dee Morton wasn't at the bus stop all winter.

The last morning in February she stood in the tooth-cracking cold. She wore a long gray cape. An unlit cig hung off her lip. Her eyebrows were tweezed to thin arches. Her eyes were circled with black. Her blond locks were chopped off in a shag. She wore no hat. Her ears stuck out pink.

I squinted in her direction.

She pocketed the cig and got on the school bus.

On Tuesday morning she lit the cigarette. On Wednesday morning she stared at nothing. On Thursday morning I looked in her direction. She glared back. On Friday morning I walked up and opened my mouth. Nothing came out. She rolled her eyes and got on the bus. My heart fell into my gut.

That afternoon after the bus dropped us off I spoke.

"Dee-dee?"

She kept walking up the slope.

I was going to ask, whatever happened to those Poison Pens? Did she know they were still being written? Did she get more herself? Had she deduced the culprit?

"Dee-dee."

She kept walking.

"DEE-DEE!"

She stopped but did not turn around.

"Whatever happened—?" I asked.

She turned to me.

Her eyes had gone milky.

The wrong words came out of my mouth.

"Whatever happened to all those yellowed letters?"

She cracked a grin, "Our yellowed letters? Oh Cat. Did you really believe all that crap?"

Uphill she turned, her gray cape dragging.

Spit rose in my throat.

All that crap?

What did she mean?

All our yellowed letters—?

The perfumed softness, smoothed by long ago hands? *All that crap?* Had Dee-dee written those yellowed letters? Had she crumpled the paper and steeped them in tea and used an old fountain pen to scratch out the shivery cursive? Had she composed the love-notes to Mush Boy and Tess? And the letters of the murderous Blacksmith? Did she rub them in perfume and drip saltwater through an eyedropper? Had she spidered her fingers into the crack of our front steps to place that first yellowed note?

And did she hide all the others, in the haunted truck, the storm sewer, the ice house, and practically every other crack in White Rock?

Hot tears blurred the road.

I swallowed, looking up.

From high over White Rock in that tooth-cracking-cold, the truth came crashing down.

Dee-dee had faked the yellowed letters.

She faked every single one.

What else had she faked?

The deadly crank call?

We're gonna kill you, kill your mom, and kill your sister.

Had she faked our time travel? And killing the Evil Blacksmith? Had she smeared that sword with fake blood? Had she lied about going back in time to the Black Bone Tavern?

But hadn't I traveled back? Hadn't I seen that Voyageur and his artifacts? Hadn't I stood in the snow with my bare feet and watched him vomit?

Yes I had.

Dee-dee faked it. She'd faked it all. She faked the yellowed letters and faked the time travel and faked the love. But I hadn't faked it. I'd stood barefoot in the snow of Little Rose before civilization bloodied the land, and I'd seen vomit spew from the Voyageur's mouth, and saw the statuettes of Fat Lady and Lion Man, and I'd loved Dee-dee. I'd loved Dee-dee as hard as a person could love. But as she disappeared around the curve with her gray cape dragging, I knew I'd never love Dee-dee Morton again.

Part Three

Catastrophe

TWENTY-ONE

"We hafta do it now, Cat."

Stringbean's nose was pressed to our living room window as she chomped Hubba Bubba and watched Mr. Anderson get his ice house off.

Stringbean and I had been watching the lake. We were watching for the skating to stop, the hockey pucks to sink, and the ice houses to come off.

The skating had stopped, the snowdrifts had dwindled, brown grass was showing, the trees wore a haze of pink, and Mr. Anderson's ice house was the last off.

"We gotta do it today."

"No, Stringbean."

Every day Stringbean brought her ice-breaking tools, handsaw, hatchet, and sledgehammer.

And every day she breathed down my neck, chomping Hubba Bubba and saying we gotta do it now.

But our timing had to be perfect.

The mummy had waited all winter in my closet under the mound of chalk and salt, and we had to bury him discreetly, with honor, or we'd be in for a worse curse than the one I put on the vacant lot.

I'd considered a desert burial. I had a great aunt who lived in Arizona. I could bury the mummy there. But how to get him on an airplane? Perhaps he'd get lost in Baggage Claim. And that aunt never invited me anyway. We could bury the mummy in the old grave I'd dug down by the lake. But the neighbor dogs would sniff him out and lakewater would seep in and molder him. The best burial, in the Valley of the Kings, we couldn't afford. The proper thing, donating him to the Science Museum, I couldn't stomach. I didn't want the mummy trapped under glass with people staring at him all day. And when did Stringbean and I ever do the proper thing? But leaving him in my closet under all that salt and chalk wouldn't do. I felt in my gut the ancient curses descending. We needed to work fast to appease the animal-headed gods and goddesses.

I finally decided on a burial at sea (lake). A Viking burial in Little Rose. It was my mummy now and my blood was Viking blood. We'd set his precious carcass afloat in a boat, like my long-dead ancestors, then set the boat alight. What a sendoff!

But what vessel? Mr. Anderson's aluminum fishing boat wouldn't burn. Dad's old cabin cruiser was too big. The metal barrels of our raft wouldn't sink. The styrofoam floaters on Stringbean's raft would give off toxic clouds of billowing smoke. We could use my aquamarine blow-up mattress. It was small and narrow like the mummy, but when set alight it would pop, then the mummy would plop in and sink before burning.

We didn't want his mummy parts falling in unhallowed for the snappers and crayfish to feed on. We needed him to burn completely, consumed by fire—or we'd be in for serious curses. *Let not my flesh be cast into the sea, or suffer forever in burning agony!*

We had to do it right, and do it soon, and there was no boat we could sacrifice. It would have to be an ice float.

TWENTY-TWO

The crabapples were about to bloom, the green beaks of our tulips were pushing up, and Easter vacation was one day away. Soon kids would be all over our shore, rolling up their pants, exposing their winter knees, daring each other in.

No one must see our water burial.

It must be carried out in secret.

On our cold strip of sand Stringbean and I made our plan. We would act in the early hours of morning. Stringbean would sleep over. We had Mom's brightest quilt to wrap the mummy. We'd combined enough flammables (gasoline and charcoal fluid) to set the mummy alight. And we had strike-anywhere matches.

We could sneak Mr. Anderson's boat out before dawn, row to the middle, find an ice chunk, place the mummy on, soak his remains in flammable liquid and deliver our sacred burial rite as dictated by *The Egyptian Book of the Dead*, then toss the lighted match. Whoof! Up in flames! A freed soul! Fire and ice!

As the mummy burned, I'd chant more ancient prayers for the Dead, and the mummy would fry to a crisp, and the ice-chunk would melt, and his spirit would rise free, unencumbered by that caramelized body.

TWENTY-THREE

On the eve of our water burial we were too excited to sleep.

We sat in my bed talking and dipping Fritos in peppermint ice cream. Stringbean talked and I listened. She talked of crayfish and spit-bombs, and of how humungous that snapping turtle Old Joe must be after years of growing down under the muck.

She stretched out her arms, a six foot span.

"Do you think he's this big, Cat?"

I shrugged.

Old Joe hadn't been seen since we were little.

He was probably long dead, turtle soup.

Stringbean talked on about the forts we'd build, the frogs she'd catch, and the secret path from Dead End Woods to Big Snake Lake she'd show me come summer. But I wasn't going to Dead End Woods or Big Snake Lake, and I wasn't going to let any boy stick his tongue down my throat there.

I scooped ice cream into a curly Frito, feeling that familiar burn in my hips.

"Um, Stringbean, have you ever kissed a girl?"

She swallowed, "Um, no."

"Well, um, would you like to?"

"Um," she wiped her mouth, "I think I wanna kiss a boy first, see how that feels."

Fair enough, Stringbean...

By three a.m. we figured we were safe.

We could perform the secret burial and not be seen, but we had to move fast, before light dawned.

We snuck downhill in the dark with the ice-breaking tools, then snuck down again with the mummy, carefully wrapped in the brightest of Mom's quilts, and double-protected with two plastic trash bags.

The lake was still as we carried the bundle past our towering birdhouse, past Mrs. Anderson's clothesline full of square dance petticoats, and past the grinning heads of the Northern Pikes.

The dock groaned as we stepped on.

"Shh! They'll hear us!"

"No they won't."

"Yes they will."

Perhaps Mr. Anderson was rising for an early-morning cast? Or Mrs. Anderson would come out for her dewy petticoats?

"Come on!" Stringbean said. "We should push off!"

We hunched on the dock, trying to maneuver the mummy.

"You go first."

"No, the head should be at the head."

"So?"

"So which is the head?"

"You have the head, Cat!"

"No, I mean which is the bow?"

"You know which is the bow!"

I knew, but it was hard to see.

"Turn round."

"We can't."

We had to turn around back on land.

Once again on the dock, we discovered a new problem. How to fit in the gear without again beheading the mummy?

In the near-darkness we had to empty the boat of Mr. Anderson's buckets and nets. There was water in the bottom. I felt it, cold and wet.

"I'm not setting the mummy in that!"

"Bail it out then!"

"What with?"

We saw nothing but full minnow buckets.

"Soak it up then."

"With what?"

"The clothes-line square-dance stuff!"

"No, Stringbean!"

"Then just put it in."

"I'm not putting the mummy in that water."

"He'll be plenty wet soon."

I shook my head. "First he'll burn."

"He's wrapped in plastic, Cat. Just put him in."

"He's too holy to get wet. And if he gets wet he won't burn. Stay and guard him. I'll be right back."

I ran uphill in the pre-dawn.

Stringbean started after.

I hissed, "Stay with the mummy!"

She ran back down, then shouted, "CRAP!"

Did her yell wake everyone on Little Rose?

No lights went on, that I could see. I went in our back door, grabbed an armload of beach towels, then heard Dad cough upstairs.

"That you kiddo?"

I held my breath.

"Kiddo?"

"Yes Dad?"

"Why up so early?"

"Um."

Truth is always best.

I climbed the stairs to whisper.

"We're taking Mr. Anderson's boat out for a Viking burial."

Dad coughed into his elbow, nodding me off.

Ten kids, he'd heard everything.

Back down in the gray dawn Stringbean was pacing the dock.

"We can't do this, Cat."

"Yes we can. We have to."

"No. We should just drop him here."

She pointed towards the end of the dock, where Mr. Anderson had sunk years of Christmas trees as welcoming shade for the northerns.

" Here. Just dump him."

"No! He has to be burned before entering the lake."

"Uh."

She stared down at me as I sopped up water.

"I mean it, Stringbean."

We loaded the mummy, but he felt funny. Wobbly in the head. No time to worry, we loaded the gear and got on.

Stringbean rowed, the oars creaking.

"Don't hit the sides!"

"I'm not!"

"Yes you are!"

"I'm not trying to!"

As she rowed I tried to keep my feet off our precious cargo. It was crowded in there with the gas cans, ice-breaking tools, and Stringbean's long legs, but the lake was mostly open, with a few ice chunks, some small as paperbacks, some large as blankets.

I shivered.

A pale tinge appeared in the east.

"Get a move-on!"

"I'm rowing fast as I can!"

Near the middle I saw it. Glowing-pink. A perfect chunk.

"There!"

"Where?"

"Don't look. Keep rowing. I'll tell you when to stop."

She gave a few more pulls.

"Now. Let it glide."

Stringbean rested the oars. They dripped on the mummy. I cringed. I wanted a perfect burial. This was messy.

We bumped against the float. The chunk was oblong, not too wide, air mattress size. On that ice, soaked in gasoline, the mummy would burn, then the ice would melt, and the remains would sink, freed to ash.

No time to spare! The first stripe of sunrise.

"Okay. Careful."

We squeezed our legs aside and gingerly lifted the bundle. Something wasn't right. As I held the bony shoulders, the head wobbled, unnaturally loose.

Stringbean had a sick look as she lifted the foot.

"Just put it on, Cat. It's getting light."

"I see that. But first we have to take off the bags."

We slid off the black plastic Hefties.

There was Mom's quilt of entangled ecstasy, there the blessed bundle. But the head was moving. Was it coming alive? Perhaps all this wetness was bringing the mummy back to life!

Stringbean put her head down and swallowed.

I knew that look.

"Stringbean, what have you done?"

"Sorry. I, uh, when you were up getting the towels, I, uh, slipped on the dock. I hit the, I stepped on the—"

Her voice squeaked.

"On, on, the, the—"

My voice went hard. "On the what, Stringbean?"

"Sorry Cat, I couldn't help it."

"You stepped on the what?"

"I tripped on the head! Sorry!"

Just then the first bird of morning—

Twoo-weet!

We were done for. No time for perfection now. We hauled the wrapped mummy from the boat with its wobbling head, eased it on the ice, cast the gasoline, hastily lit matches, and threw them toward the float.

Some matches fell hissing to the water.

Some sizzled out on the ice.

One hit the mummy's chest and blazed.

We held our breath, watching the mummy burn, then nearly caught fire ourselves when a spill of gasoline on Stringbean's sweatshirt sleeve caught flame.

I grabbed her wrist and sunk it in the lake, almost tipping the boat as the blaze heated our faces, glowing us orange, tingeing the mist pale tangerine.

We could not linger.

We had to get that boat back. And soon.

And we had to stay and watch the fire.

And what about the chanting? I'd memorized pages and pages of ancient phrases to ensure the mummy's proper transition into eternity.

Let not the dark ones find me…
Let not the Soul-eaters eat me…
Let the rays of great Ra embrace me—

"Let the goddess of Earth and the god of Sky enfold me," I chanted as the sun rose glimmering over Little Rose and the Great Blue Heron took flight and the mummy burned on his chunk and the great sun blinded us and the fire went out on the dwindling float and the ice broke and our mummy fell, PLOP, headless, into the water.

We had to use the oar to jab the head in.

What a mess! Now snappers would eat his remains, and bullheads would feed on his heart, and frogs would dart through his privates, and crayfish would nest in the hollow of his dismembered head as the curses for anyone who defaced a mummy grabbed hold of us. We were EFFED.

TWENTY-FOUR

We got the boat back in time to avoid trouble.

I piled the sopping towels in our basement, carried the gas cans back to our garage, and repaired the burn on Stringbean's sweatshirt with an iron-on patch as I tried not to think about the mummy down there disintegrating in the muck with the wavering crayfish.

That night I dreamed of the mummy as he was in my sleepover dream, that night I tangled in the sheets with Dee-dee.

There was the dream as before.

There was mermaid Dee-dee in the chalk canoe.

There she was on the steps of the old apartment. There in the rooms full of boxes, there discovering the mummy, there dipping the tissue and bringing the mummy back to life. And there was mermaid Dee-dee ending her tale in my perfect chalk canoe as the sky cracked with thunder—

One loud CRACK!

I shot up in bed in a sea of sweat.

In my dream the sky had cracked.

The question the cops asked us that horrible morning came back. Did you hear the gunshot? I said no, I didn't hear a gunshot. But I was dead wrong. I did hear the gunshot. I heard it in my dream. As Robbie Morton in the basement held the gun to his head and pulled the trigger, my dream sky cracked with thunder.

Then I realized.

I should have drowned Dee-dee.

In my dream I should have drowned her. When she crested the water, I should have put my hand on her head and pushed down. Could have. Should have. For the act of killing in dreams always wakes me. I could have woken, run downstairs and kicked the gun away before Robbie pulled the trigger.

Too late.

The next day I got my first Poison Pen.

Cat McCloud,

I saw what you did. You and that godless tomboy. I saw you disposing of a body! NOW YOU WILL BURN IN HELL. But first you will ROT IN PRISON. Then you will FRY IN THE ELECTRIC CHAIR. Then you will BURN IN HELL.

TWENTY-FIVE

Every day after that I watched out my bedroom window.

My heart beat to escape my ribs as I peered through my blinds waiting for the cops to come handcuff me and throw me in prison for desecrating a mummy.

No cops ever came.

The ice went out, the leaves unfurled, the crabapples flaunted their whorish beauty, and the lawnmowers rumbled in summer, with its heat, its sweat, and endless sunbathing slathered in Coppertone.

June and July sizzled by with sand in my hair, sand in my toes, and muggy nights filled with fantasies of boys and girls touching me, then I'd wake to the coppery taste of disintegrating mummy.

He was still down there headless in the muck. I imagined the mummy in the deepest of Little Rose, wavering with his softened tissues beside the long-lost artifacts of the Voyageur, the Fat Lady and the Lion Man.

I imagined Fat Lady and Lion Man bumping against the mummy's privates and propagating deadly curses for my horrific demise.

Let not my head be lost from me.
For I have come at the wish of my heart—
From the Pool of Double Fire—

And when the sky weeps—
I shall wash the heart of Heaven with my Wrath!
The Book of the Dead was always with me that summer, Dee-dee's sunhat was always on my head, and something was about to explode.

I felt the dread swelling as I lay baking down at the lake, squinting at the hieroglyphics in Book of the Dead, while on the other side of the freeway wall the wild teens on the shores of Big Snake partied with their dangerous flirting, tongue-kissing, and breast-squeezing.

July passed like a swoon.
Like Osiris shooting light from the flame of his mouth—
And the empty page of my notebook glared at me, greasy with suntan oil. I was still trying to answer Dad's old questions.
Who are you, what are you doing, what do you want to be doing?
I'm a ball of deadness. I'm doing nothing.
I want to float forever in a bubble of nothing.

Then came Stockyard Days of 1974. A parade in downtown White Rock, marching bands, contests, booths, and music, all mixed with the smells of burning flesh and dusty sweat. A steer was roped in the parking lot of Howie's Meats, a team of Clydesdales stomped outside Blue Moon Ballroom, and red, white, and blue streamers were draped on the First State Bank. There was square dancing by the post office. The Andersons showed off their fanciest moves, and the dentist gave out suckers—the little kid kind with the looped holder so you didn't gouge your throat when you fell down.

In late afternoon I left the noisy commemoration and went down to Little Rose Lake. Everyone else was still at Stockyard Days. They'd come back soon to barbeque. And after the sun set, the firemen on the shores of Big Snake would ready the gunpowder rockets. Then Mom and Dad would paddle our raft out, disrobe in the dark and slip into the lake naked. And Mr. and Mrs. Anderson would row their aluminum boat out. And the Blakes would crowd onto their pontoon, the adults with cocktails, the kids with popsicles. And the Zupinskis would paddle out in their red canoe, Mrs. Zupinski with her trusty binoculars, to watch the fireworks reflected in Little Rose.

But the fireworks never happened that year.

That afternoon, as I swam my air mattress into the middle, Little Rose was dead-still. Nothing moved. No lawnmowers hummed. No kids ran down. No boats roared.

I had the whole lake to myself.

I floated in the middle with Dee-dee's sunhat over my face. My hands trailed in the cool water. The sun heated my thighs. The inside of Dee-dee's hat smelled of warm straw and Dee-dee.

In that dark heat, the sun broke through every pinhole, a thousand globes of light.

Always before, as I lay under Dee-dee's hat, each pinhole was empty, a tiny burning sun. But today in that sweet darkness, within each sun was a creature in silhouette, black against gold.

In one globe was a tiny black crow.

In another a mermaid. In another a girl—

Spider, boy, brontosaurus, Great Blue Heron, snake, dog, leaping fish. Every creature of the earth was inside Dee-dee's hat, encased in its own golden droplet, getting ready to be born and burst forth. Then the sky darkened and all the creatures disappeared.

TWENTY-SIX

Everyone remembers where they were when the tornado hit.

I was floating in the middle of Little Rose. Stringbean was on her beach hugging her inner tube. Sassy Melody was in a lawn chair painting her toenails. The Blake boys were strapping on life vests. Flipper was untangling a fishing line. Zipper was peering into his minnow bucket. The bratty twins were sneaking down between houses.

Mrs. Zupinski was on her patio stirring potato salad. Mom was stepping out our back door to check on the rotisserie chicken. Holly was stirring a pitcher of lemonade.

Mrs. Blake was calling her girls up to help with the relish-trays. Mrs. Green put down her poodle and picked up her watermelon knife. Mrs. Anderson, in her square-dancing skirts, stepped out her back door with a cherry pie, noticed a windfall apple, set down the pie and bent for the apple. The back of her skirt rose in a jubilation of petticoats—

The sky went green.

The blue jays fell silent.

The grasshoppers stopped singing.

Dogs and cats froze mid-scratch. The only sound the spitting of grills and grinding of rotisseries. All the neighbors stopped turning meat and looked up.

Mrs. Zupinski set the potato salad spoon too close to the picnic table edge and it clattered to the cement. Mr. Blake dropped the ice cube tray to the grass. Zipper jerked his hand from the minnow bucket and the bucket tipped, freeing some minnows to flip in the water and some to die on the dock.

Holly let go of our lemonade pitcher.

It shattered to the flagstones.

Then the mayflies came. By the millions. Clouds of mayflies hovered over Little Rose. I'd never seen mayflies anywhere but on the Mississippi, but here they were, on the sand, covering the tree trunks, and hovering over the water.

Hatch, mate, and die.

One landed on my arm.

I flicked it off.

Then the siren.

TORNADO!

The Blake girls calf-deep covered their ears. The bratty twins turned and ran home. Mrs. Zupinski rushed in her potato salad. All the neighbors hurried to the northwest corner of their basements, grabbing ripple chips and whiskey on the way and turning their radios to WCCO.

The spitting T-bones, hamburgers, and hot dogs on the grills blackened with the hissing bratwurst and sassing drumsticks. Our rotisserie chicken had just then reached perfection, the meat falling off the bone, perfect, melt-in-your-mouth chicken.

I never got to eat one bite of that.

I flicked off another mayfly, rolled from the air mattress and began to swim home. Stringbean was still hugging her inner tube. Mom hurried round our house with the ladder and climbed to the roof with a drink in her hand to watch the show. Dad, despite his arthritic knees, came running after.

Mayflies hovered over all.

At first they flew haphazardly, but later, when the third after-wind hit, the mayflies would fly in formation, their millions of tiny brown bodies all facing into the wind.

I felt the change in air pressure.

Then heard it—

A train speeding down Highlook.

Then saw it, cracking houses, exploding stucco, shattering glass. Gutter pipes, bicycles, and lawnmowers catapulted.

WHUMP! Uprooted trees hit parked cars.

WHUMP! Birdfeeders hit barbeques.

WHUMP! Plaster gnomes hit picture windows.

From the middle of Little Rose Lake I saw the twister nick Carters' roof, spitting shingles, sending their grill into a spin, and knocking over our rotisserie.

Dee-dee's hat flew from my head.

Hamburgers spiraled, steaks boomeranged, shingles skipped on the water.

I ducked a drumstick.

A shingle struck my shoulder.

A shard from Holly's lemonade pitcher found my cheek.

The twister rose, then dipped, whipping the top of our birdhouse, sending it spiraling, splintering the crack in the pole made last summer by Zipper Zupinski. The widened crack zig-zagged like lightning down the thirty-foot birdhouse pole.

The twister hovered.

Was it coming towards me? Or rising up?

I was too far out to swim in.

Mom and Dad rushed down the ladder.

I filled my lungs and dove deep.

I swam down but went up, in a nightmare of going nowhere. I fought the uprushing waters with all my powers, set my jaw, and aimed ferociously for the bottom, down, down.

Instead of my fingers sinking into useless muck, my hands slid over an outboard motor.

Blakes' lost Evinrude! Still attached to their sunken boat.

Avoiding the deadly propeller fins, I side-grasped the shaft and held on as the waters rose, an inverted Niagara.

The up-rush lifted me feet-first. The motor held fast to the boat. The boat stuck fast in the muck. Little Rose rushed past my ears, exploding from my nose, peeling back my lips, tearing off my bikini-bottoms. I squeezed my lids shut to keep my eyeballs from popping out.

My fingers, strong from carving, were losing their grip.

The waters gave a great upward suck.

The sunken boat shivered, jerked, and rose.

I clung to the motor shaft, head down, feet up, in an oblivion of air. I no longer felt rushing water around me, but chill air.

CLUNK!

The boat, motor, and I were dropped to the muck.

My chin hit the Evinrude.

I opened my eyes to a sight never seen.

All of Little Rose Lake was sucked empty. Every drop twistered up. I un-grasped the shaft and turned side-to-side. The twister had left just a bowl of muck and muck-covered humps. The muck slid from the humps, revealing lost things.

A toilet bowl. A baby-doll. A swim-fin.

I stepped towards the baby-doll and sank knee-deep. More muck slid away, revealing a tennis shoe, a turtle shell, a car tire.

Then a gasp.

Stringbean, on her end, her long limbs wrapped round a dock piling, her bikini bottoms also sucked off.

I headed towards her, but slowed by the muck, cupped my hands and shouted.

"STRINGBEAN! YOU OKAY?"

She panted, hugging the piling.

"STRINGBEAN?"

She coughed. Water gushed from her mouth.

"Ah!"

She gasped, fell to the muck, and was instantly clothed in gray-green. She cast her arms wide.

"Cat! Do you see what I see?"

"Yes, Stringbean, I see!"

Our dream had come true! The bottom was laid bare. There was a muddied Barbie, there my brown trike, there an old washing machine. There the skeleton of a Model T.

All around us covered in muck were lost things. Alarm clock. Once-red wagon. Wooden sled. Beach ball. Rusty rifle. Box spring. Toaster. Tin soldier. Somewhere buried in this muck were my sisters' lost wedding rings.

I waved at Mom and Dad, safe on the ground, too storm-shocked to wave back, then Stringbean and I threw ourselves into the muck, laughing and whooping as we schlooked through, pulling up treasure after treasure, holding each aloft, and schlooking on to pull up more.

What was that? Pearl necklace! Boat cushion! Jello-mold! Dishrack! Prom dress! Whatever color it was once was, it was muck-green now. Cross-your-heart bra, muck-green too. Sunglasses, soup-can, unopened jar of sauerkraut!

We pulled up familiar stuff—broomsticks, beach balls, a walkie-talkie, a Hot Wheels, a jack-in-the-box.

Then older stuff started bubbling up. Cast iron bed, wooden wagon wheel, bear trap, ball-and-chain. And bottles. Whiskey bottles, wine bottles, baby bottles, milk bottles, bottle after bottle, some so old and thick they must have come from back when this was an outpost.

The muck on the shorelines slid down, revealing old tree roots. In the exposed roots, preserved perfectly as ancient bodies in Danish peat bogs, were creatures. A wire-hair terrier. A Great Blue Heron. A beaver. And that huge thing? A bison?

More mud along the banks slid free, exposing copper-colored people hammocked in the roots of trees. A woman curled as if in the womb, her long hair striping her shoulder. A man curled in another, his buckskin sleeve the same bronze as his face. And in the roots by the storm sewer, three small children entangled in a sleeping embrace.

I struggled towards the children, then saw my Voyageur, just as he'd been the night of my time travel. But rather than buried in snow, he was buried in muck, his wooly hat, furry collar, and grizzled face all muck-laden.

I fought my way to the old stone foundation, dropped to my knees, and dug beside the Voyageur.

What happened to his pouch of statuettes?

Muck filled my fingernails, swallowed my legs, and sucked at my arms.

Stringbean hollered, "Cat, look at this!!"

She held up a lost croquet mallet.

I kept digging. Wary of another bear trap or a buried snapper, my fingers reached into the slippery unseen.

I felt sticks, tiny bones, old leather.

I closed my fist and drew it up—

The little pouch!

The first of the back-winds hit as I forced two fingers in.

Out came disintegrating leaves, a wee crayfish, then the nubbly head, ginormous breasts, and protuberant belly of the Fat Venus. The second after-wind hit as I thrust my fingers deeper, drawing out the small head, ivory locks, and muzzle of the Lion Man. I spit both artifacts clean, grasped one in each hand, and struggled to stand.

As I held my treasures aloft, lost bats flitted over the lakebed, the back doors of the houses opened, and out came all the neighbors to the sight-never-seen.

Out came sassy Melody with her frosty-pink nails. Out came Stringbean's mom and dad in their BBQ aprons. Out came the neighborhood dogs and cats sniffing for windblown meats.

Carter's chihuahua fought over a T-bone with Mrs. Green's poodle, as out came Mr. and Mrs. Anderson in their square dance clothes. Out came the Blake kids, prancing and dancing, picking up downed branches and waving them like Isadora Duncans. Even the neighbors with the chain link fence came out to stare at the missing lake, and out came Zipper and Flipper Zupinski, cartwheeling down the hill.

Zipper and Flipper stopped at the edge of the muck and gaped. Behind them came Mr. Zupinski with a minnow bucket. Holly came out squeezing her finger, pierced by a shard of lemonade pitcher. I felt my cheek, where a flying shard had cut.

Out stepped Mrs. Zupinski with her trusty binoculars. She locked the binoculars to her eyes, intent on the wreckage. She trained her spyglass on the muck. The gasping fish. The barking dogs, the dancing kids. Mrs. Zupinski's big red mouth opened and shut like a landed bullhead as she turned this way and that, spying the destruction. Cat fights. Storm-thrown barbeques. The hole in Blakes' roof.

Stringbean's mom and dad threw their arms around each other and kissed. Mom and Dad hugged. Mrs. Green rubbed noses with her poodle. The dancing kids on the shore rolled all over each other, their muck-covered arms and legs entangling, as frogs hopped, bats flicked, Carter's chihuahua humped the Blake's cat, and one painted turtle mounted another.

Mr. Zupinski rushed uphill to kiss his wife—

Before he reached her, Mrs. Zupinski lowered her binoculars

and found her voice:

"SINNERS!" she shouted.

Mr. Zupinski stopped running.

The entangled kids fell silent.

Mom and Dad froze.

All eyes went to Mrs. Zupinski.

"BLASPHEMERS!" she roared, "BLASPHEMERS ALL! THIS IS WHAT COMES OF LIVING IN SIN!"

Mr. Zupinski put out a hand to quiet her.

Her eyes were mad with venom. Or was it fear?

"NOW YOU SHALL ALL BURN IN HELL!"

Then the third after-wind came. The third after-wind came stiff, sending strings of spit straight-line from Mrs. Zupinski's open mouth and blowing the hovering mayflies into formation, their little brown bodies all facing into the wind.

That stiff wind took a final crack at the fault-line in the thirty-foot pole of our birdhouse, ripped a jagged break, tipped the pole sideways, and arrowed it straight towards the heart of Mrs. Zupinski.

TWENTY-SEVEN

The shaft buried itself in Mrs. Zupinski's chest.

She clutched at the shaft and sank to the lawn.

Mr. Zupinski threw down his bucket and ran to her. Zipper and Flipper raced uphill to their mom.

Stuck calf-deep in muck, with Fat Venus and Lion Man in my upraised hands, I watched the Zupinskis collapse around their wife and mother. The approaching sirens drowned out their cries. No one else moved but the growling dogs and hissing cats.

The sky filled with torn scraps of black paper. The shore went black with crows. The air turned heavy, fish-scented.

A great roaring came from above.

A frog fell to the muck.

I looked up.

A yellow-green column of water descended.

I cracked my jaw, "STRINGBEAN, RUN!"

Adrenalin spurted her homeward but I couldn't move. I could only look up as all of Little Rose Lake rushed toward me.

At the last moment I tucked my chin.

The column of water hit hard, ripping Fat Lady and Lion Man from my hands, knocking out my wind, clacking my teeth, jamming me down, and burying me upright in the deepest of Little Rose.

The returning waters churned but didn't dislodge me.

Belly-deep in muck under thirty feet of lakewater, I tried to worm my way out.

I would not budge.

Here was a muck-hole like no other, and no neighbor kids to pull me from this.

I'd laugh, if laughing didn't quicken my death.

You know that feeling like you're dying when you're really only just waking up? That pain in your pumper like your insides are about to turn inside out and the dams of your arteries are about to give way and all that you've been holding in is about to explode into the unknown? Death has a taste. It bubbles up from the inside, black and green, thick and sour, a grainy mush. I almost drowned once before, when the bratty twins who couldn't swim used me as a ladder, so I know how death-by-drowning feels. The white circle of water closing over, your last look at sky, that delicious fishy smell and the silent scream that brings in more water. And I've tasted death in my dreams, in the back of my throat while cleaning out the endlessly overflowing public toilets of Sleepland. But this is real life. In real life when death spills out of you in a pudding mush, then you know you were carrying death around inside you all that time. You were letting death walk upright inside you.

I used to think death was on the outside waiting for me. I used to think death was around the corner as I toddled from our bedroom and Holly jumped out and yelled BOO! At every corner Holly waited like death trying to scare me out of my rubber pants. And death was in the copper oven, and the grinning Northern Pike heads nailed to the trees, and in the fine point of the exacto knife cutting into me, and in Dee-dee's eyes and the missing back of Robbie Morton's head and around every corner and under every bed and in every crack waiting to jump out, say BOO and—

Slow down, I told myself. Slow your heartbeat like in your underwater breathing contests with Stringbean. The slower your heartbeat, the less air you need. What do you need right now? You need A DEEPER SELF AWARENESS. What were those questions Dad brought home from his conference?

WHO ARE YOU?

That was the first question.

Who am I?

The answer is not a fourteen year old weirdo named Cat McCloud about to drown in White Rock Minnesota in the middle of the expanding universe.

I'm none of those tiny chewable bits.

I'm a being composed of cells free to be whatever the EFF I want to be. And the more I fight it, the worse off I'll be.

Remember Mermaid School. Your days underwater. Mermaids can breathe down here. They don't need to come up for air. Mermaids can relax, chill out, and draw oxygen from the water into their cells through the sheer force of love.

Shoulders, arms, and hands, relax.

Toes, feet, and legs, relax.

Relax as deeply as you'll be if you ever get another chance to kiss Dee-dee.

If I ever got another chance to kiss Dee-dee, I'd slide my tongue in so deep it would come out her other end—

Then here she is before me. Dee-dee in the yellow-green water. Her skin palest jade. Her locks wavering. Her breasts floating. Dee-dee is a mermaid, so close I see the hairs on her arms, the goosebumps on her belly, and the glint of her scales.

She takes my face in her hands.

Her mouth bubbles.

"I am crazy-mad about you, Cat."

She gives me a grinding kiss. Her scales cut my thighs. Her fingers squeeze my nipple.

I'm fainting.

Dee-dee, you'll have to wake me again with a kiss!

I put my arms around her.

Her back is hard and bumpy. Her mouth is a beak. Her eyes are slits. She's big around as a hula hoop.

This isn't Dee-dee. This is Old Joe, the giant snapping turtle, come to bite off my face.

I twist.

Twisting pushes me deeper. Struggling uses up oxygen. Still I raise my arms and wriggle.

I don't budge.

Old Joe bumps my side, searching for purchase. He works up my body. Poke-poke. Bump-bump.

On my right wrist he sinks home.

The worst pain ever.

TUG! Old Joe tugs.

My body lurches but doesn't budge.

Old Joe re-grips both wrists, locks his pointed jaws in my flesh, and retugs.

The worst pain just got worse.

His tugs strengthen the suction.

Lungs on fire, I'll breathe water soon.

The lost mummy-head floats by, trailing strips of flesh.

I feel a scuttling at my feet, a tickling-scratching. The tickling-scratching covers my buried toes. The tickling-scratching works up my buried calves. The tickling-scratching surrounds my buried thighs up to my privates. From toes to belly I'm wrapped in tickling-scratching.

Old Joe is motionless above, clamping my wrists, as numberless scuttlers pinch and tickle below. Mad tickling, ten thousand fingers, all the drowned of Little Rose with their pinches, inviting me down, to sip muck from lost teacups.

I know what that tickling is.

That tickling is not drowned souls. That tickling is crayfish. All the crayfish in Little Rose come to feast on my flesh as Old Joe waits above with his vice-grip.

What are you waiting for Old Joe? For my lungs to explode? For the crayfish to pierce a thousand holes? For my wrists to snap off and death to come billowing out in two great red exclamation marks?

The nibbling frenzy increases.

The crayfish aren't eating me. They're weakening the suction.

One more tickle of tiny claw.

A sliding under my toes.

The suction breaks.

Up I rush, with Old Joe towing.

Up, up—

A final jerk of his neck.

The white circle opens.

I choke on air.

Old Joe has dragged me near the far shore.

I swim coughing towards the old ice house foundation. The water blackens. I raise my hands, kicking to stay up. Along with my punctured wrists, my right hand geysers blood. Old Joe bit off the tip of my eff you finger.

I swim one-armed.

My feet find the mushy bottom. I stumble ashore bare-assed, coughing lakewater, fountaining blood. Landed fish gasp amid downed branches, burger wrappers, and Dee-dee's battered sunhat. I wriggle from my bikini top and wrap it round my gushing finger, using my teeth to pull tight.

My blood slows to a glug.

I lean naked against the old stone foundation to catch my breath. As my blood grows sticky and my heartbeat slows, the sky opens over Little Rose, clear and blue, and the creatures return. The Great Blue Heron dips its neck. The crows caw at the lost bats. The bratty twins sneak down between houses. Mom and Dad stare up at our broken birdhouse shaft. Stringbean does a crazy monkey dance. Mr. Anderson bends over his boat.

And across the sky words appear. The words that were hiding in me. The words that would never come up. The words I'd wanted to say to Robbie Morton as he cried at his desk, and cried at recess, and cried on those poison pens the night he put a gun to his head. Those words write themselves across the sky.

Robbie Morton,

Go ahead and cry. Bust your throat crying. Cry for every damned person on this lake, for deep inside we're all sobbing our guts out.

The words dissolve. I vomit up a green mush. And a minnow. I vomit a minnow up. Still alive, it flips back in the water. With my budding breasts encased in blood and my privates caked in muck, I look out over the lake—and see death everywhere. Death in the fish spit out by the storm, death in the downed branches and the sod peeled back and the shattered windows and uprooted trees, and death in Zipper and Flipper sobbing over their mom. And death in all the mayflies covering the water. I'll have to swim back home through those little corpses.

But as I look out over the lake I see something else. In the light on the water, in the sheen of Mr. Anderson's boat as he puts it back in, in the legs of the bratty kids running back down, in their pumping knees and screaming throats and bratty sass, and in the pimples of the big boys and girls waiting for me on the other side of the freeway wall at the public beach on Big Snake, in their tongues and their sweat and their elbows and their hidden body parts throbbing and their transistor radios saying *this is KDWB 63 with your hit parade*, I see life. Life in every creature waiting around every corner to jump out, say BOO, and scare me out of my skin.

TWENTY-EIGHT

Next morning I wake with my sewn finger throbbing. Mom stands over me with a pillowcase full of tiny bumps. She dumps the pillowcase out on my bed. Tink! Out come all my chalk canoes, all my brokens with their dots of blood. Mom says do you know why you carved so many? I shrug. You carved them because they were difficult, she says. If they were easy you wouldn't have done it. *Yeah right*. Mom smooths the sheet with those hands of hers, weathered from years of hard work, and covered in tiny scars, like little mouths keeping secrets. Then Mom speaks the words those scars had been holding in all along. When I was a girl, she says, my mother put me to work carving a chalk canoe too. Just as I did you. And her mother before her. And hers before her. All we girls as far back as it goes. We carved in the night and carved in the day and all winter long. But we never could carve a perfect one, Cat. Each canoe broke in our hands—on the verge of perfection—because with this chalk and that blade, it's impossible. *Impossible?* I sit up in bed and sweep those brokens to the floor. Mom helps me stand. I raise my fists and stomp with my bare feet. Mom stomps too. We stomp those chalk canoes to bits. We stomp and stomp every little bloody one to dust. *Because that is what we think of perfection.*

ACKNOWLEDGEMENTS

Thanks to Miriam Arneson for the first chalk canoe. Thanks to Nancy Kohlsaat for the summer adventures. Thanks to Cindy Miller for the first yellowed note. Thanks to Alan Musielewicz for the long-ago gift of *The Egyptian Book of the Dead*. Thanks to Ken Varnold for the coffee breaks. Thanks to Kim Hines for the early editing advice. Thanks to Barb and Steve Coleman for the cabin writing retreats. Thanks to Rachel Anderson for the publicity. Thanks to Chad Augustin and Alberta Mirais for the cover design. Thanks also to Alberta Mirais for the exquisite illustrations and the wise editing advice. Thanks to my writing pals, Tessa Bridal, Xandra Coe and Judy Meath, and Kristen Froebel, for reading each word out loud. Your voices brought this book to life. And thanks to the Invisible Ink and Stick Pony Press team for your persistence, proof-reading, life-saving, intelligence, laughter, and support. Onward!

-Heidi Arneson, February 16, 2019

ABOUT THE AUTHOR

HEIDI ARNESON is a storyteller, author, and painter. She trail-blazed solo performance with a series of one-woman shows, created spoken word behind bars with male inmates, and plumbed the dark side of small-town secrecy in her first novel, *Interlocking Monsters*. Her plays include *Itchy Tingles*, *DeGrade School*, and *BloodyMerryJammyParty*. She is a recipient of the Bush Artist Fellowship, a Minnesota State Arts Board Artist Initiative Grant, and a Loft/Jerome Minnesota Writer's Grant.

ABOUT THE ILLUSTRATOR

ALBERTA MIRAIS is a visual artist, musician, and performer. She sings in the dance band *Fiamma*, and composes, plays keyboards, and sings in the duo *Holiday*. Her artworks of people, pets, and mythical creatures hang across the U.S. and overseas.

www.ingramcontent.com/pod-product-compliance
Lightning Source LLC
Chambersburg PA
CBHW020616120726
47905CB00003B/822